SHOULDN'T HAVE YOU

A FRACTURED CONNECTIONS NOVEL

CARRIE ANN RYAN

Shouldn't Have You
A Fractured Connections Novel
By: Carrie Ann Ryan
© 2019 Carrie Ann Ryan
ISBN: 978-1-947007-49-9

Cover Art by Charity Hendry
Photograph by Sara Eirew

For more information, please join Carrie Ann Ryan's MAILING LIST.
To interact with Carrie Ann Ryan, you can join her FAN CLUB

PRAISE FOR CARRIE ANN RYAN....

"Carrie Ann Ryan knows how to pull your heartstrings and make your pulse pound! Her wonderful Redwood Pack series will draw you in and keep you reading long into the night. I can't wait to see what comes next with the new generation, the Talons. Keep them coming, Carrie Ann!" –Lara Adrian, New York Times bestselling author of CRAVE THE NIGHT

"Carrie Ann Ryan never fails to draw readers in with passion, raw sensuality, and characters that pop off the page. Any book by Carrie Ann is an absolute treat." – New York Times Bestselling Author J. Kenner

"With snarky humor, sizzling love scenes, and brilliant, imaginative worldbuilding, The Dante's Circle series reads as if Carrie Ann Ryan peeked at my personal wish list!" – NYT Bestselling Author, Larissa Ione

DEDICATION

To Dan, first.

To those part of this odd club of ours, always:
Dani.
Ms. Bev.
Pat
Michele
Mica

Though we are never the same, I know we are not alone
because so many of you reached out. And still do.
This book is for you. And to so many more who must face
the darkness.

SHOULDN'T HAVE YOU

I've been many things in my life: daughter, friend, student, lover, wife...and now, widow. Getting past those labels and finding who I could be without them was the hardest thing I've ever done.

Then I became friends with Brendon Connolly.

Every time I look at him, I see a past, I see a present, and I'm afraid if I look too hard, I'll see a future.

I've known Harmony Wynham since before she got married. Before she lost everything. I didn't know that one day she wouldn't be just my friend but the woman I wanted to spend the rest of my life with.

Only I don't think that can happen.

Not when every time she looks at me, she sees what she lost, and I can only see what I can't overcome.

I love her, even though I shouldn't. Somehow, we need to find a balance.

Because if we don't, walking away will be the hardest thing I've ever done—even if it's the only thing I should do.

AUTHOR'S NOTE

This is not my story. This is Harmony's. I have thought long and hard if I will ever write my story, and I don't know if that time will come. But until then, this was the story I needed to write, even if it wasn't easy.

There is no one right way to grieve. Nor is there a reason you should grieve in just one way.

I didn't.

Harmony didn't.

I wrote the book that comes after. The book that shows that there's a happily ever after for everyone, even those who thought they already had theirs.

Again, this is not my story.

This is not the story of so many women who I have spoken to over the past months who have reached out to me. They held me even through words as they shared their grief. They loved and lost, as well.

So, while this book isn't our story, it is the story of finding a new path.

It is a story of rebirth, even after the loss.

This is Harmony's story.

CHAPTER ONE

I called you today. You didn't answer.

- Harmony to Moyer. 1 month ATE (after the end)

HARMONY

THE IDEA of dating had always been an abstract thing. As if it were something others did that I watched from afar, either knowing I'd never participate again since I'd already found my future or wondering how on earth people risked everything for a single date these days.

I was twenty-seven years old, and I was not only out of practice, but it also seemed I was out of my depth. As someone who detested not knowing what I was doing and who needed to be in control no matter what, that didn't bode well.

I was going on my first date since my husband's death. Since I'd lost Moyer.

I suppose I should have felt slightly different than I did at that moment, but it wasn't as if I could actually figure out what I was feeling. It was hard to put it all into words when, sometimes, there were no words at all.

I'd been called many things in my life: daughter, friend, lover, wife, and widow. I tried not to let those labels define me, and yet, somehow, they'd become my shield.

It was easy to put all of my anger and hurt and happiness and the breadth of my emotions into one word. Well, maybe not easy, but perhaps easier for everyone else.

Because sometimes it felt like I was Chris Pratt in that *Jurassic World* movie when he was facing off against the three velociraptors. As if I were standing just slightly bent, my arms outstretched, warding off those who would come at me.

Because it wasn't as if those who came at me were evil people. It wasn't as if they were mean or rude. Okay, perhaps they were a little rude, but everyone just wanted to make sure I was okay.

Everyone wanted to ensure that I understood that they didn't know how to take care of me. They didn't know how to help me feel better.

The thing was, if I knew what that took, maybe I would feel slightly better already.

So, yes, I was the dinosaur wrangler when it came to people and their emotions as they came at me. The widow.

I shook my head and tried to live in the moment rather than in my magical world inside my brain where I had drifted off to so many times over the past two years.

Yes, I was a widow.

But I was also Harmony Wynham née Jacobs. I was a person. A woman. And someone who needed connections.

Yes, I would probably cry and throw up later, but this was my first date with another man. And I was going to live in the moment because I had learned all too well that, sometimes, there weren't that many moments to live.

"So, you run a nonprofit?" Jason asked, smiling at me.

He really did have a beautiful smile. Perfect, white teeth, so straight that either he had been blessed by the genetic gods or he'd had an amazing orthodontist when he was a kid. I had been forced into braces in high school, something that I still hated to think about, considering that I hadn't gotten them off until *after* senior photos.

Jason, however, looked like he was genetically blessed in other ways, as well. A strong jaw, no need to hide a weak chin beneath a goatee like some were prone to do. He had shaved his face completely, not even a hint of scruff. His hair was perfectly manicured, an expensive cut with just enough styling product in it that it angled away from his brow, likely just the way he wanted.

He had bright gray irises, and long, thick lashes that framed those eyes perfectly.

And if I thought the word *perfect* when it came to him one more time, I might kick myself under the table.

He wore a gray suit that was just a hint darker than the color of his eyes, and I wondered to myself if he had done that on purpose. It wouldn't surprise me, honestly.

He hadn't picked me up, something I had been forceful about. Instead, I had met him in the parking lot and then noticed his very fancy—also silver/gray—BMW as he walked towards me.

He, like Mary Poppins herself, was practically perfect in every way.

At least that was how one of my coworkers had described Jason when she set us up on this blind date.

Yes, I was on a blind date. But as I had no idea how to actually date or show anyone that I was available to date, a blind date seemed like the perfect way to dip my toes into the water of the arena that seemed to scare me more than I cared to admit.

"Harmony?"

I smiled—not too much, not too little, just as my mother had taught me.

I patted my hair, trying to focus. "I'm sorry, I'm lost in my head." I lowered my hands, nodding. "Yes, I run a nonprofit for charity. It's to help local women's shelters as well as shelters for families." I didn't get paid because I had my own money. Moyer had left me well-off, and I still had my trust fund from my family. But I worked long hours and put my entire soul, or at least what was left of it, into making sure that our charity and nonprofit did the best we possibly could. Because there were so many people in need. So many women who needed help. So many females and families who had nowhere else to turn.

"That's wonderful." Jason winced, and I nodded, understanding what he meant by the action. "I meant that what you're doing is wonderful, not the fact that it's needed."

"I know. Well, at least I try to do my best. Sometimes, you can't help everyone, but as long as there's breath in my body, I'm going to make sure I can help as many people as I can."

"Well, you're pretty brilliant. At least that's what your

friends say. So I think if there is anybody who can help the entire world, it would be you."

I held back a wince of my own. That was pretty strong, or maybe just a little overdramatic. But this was a first date. It had been so long since I had been on one, perhaps this is what you did now.

I tried to remember what my first date with Moyer had been like, and I couldn't. Not really. It'd just been a movie after a long day, and then we had kissed, and that was it. Not it, but more like just the beginning of a new phase in our relationship. We had been friends, and then lovers, and then husband and wife. It had just progressed naturally.

Dating, even when I wasn't looking for a future exactly, was interesting.

I wasn't looking for a new husband. God, no. I'd had that, loved and lost and done all of the clichés. Now, I just didn't want to be lonely anymore.

Maybe I missed sex, but it had been so long that perhaps I didn't. I had myself for that. I just missed companionship. I missed a lot.

And I didn't want to be lonely anymore.

Hence this date with Jason, which was going nicely, and which I wouldn't mess up by talking about Moyer.

I needed to stop thinking about him.

Because I loved Moyer. I loved him with every ounce

of my being and would continue to love him until the day I died, and then likely into the moments after when I found what came once you closed your eyes for the last time. But I couldn't only live for that love that no longer had another end.

"So, Clarisse was saying that you own your own business?" I wasn't sure *what* that business was since she'd been vague, but asking was a good step in the right direction of initiating conversation.

He nodded and then looked down at his phone as it vibrated. He had done that a few times tonight, and I was a little worried but not too offended. My phone was buzzing in my purse beside my water glass, as well. But unless it was an emergency, I wouldn't answer. I knew the emergency vibrations, and so far, it was only simple texts. They would call if they needed me. My friends would call if they needed me.

"Yes, sorry," Jason said, setting down his phone. He had the grace to blush, and yet again, I didn't blame him. I worked long hours, and from what Clarisse had said, so did Jason. And if we were just two busy people trying to go on a date, phone calls and texts were bound to happen.

"Anyway, we're in the middle of a huge deal right now, and it's getting a little dicey. The guys on the other end are taking their time and trying to change things, and it's making my job a little harder. But I'm trying to focus. Very sorry."

I shook my head quickly and then took a sip of my wine. Crisp with pear hints. The perfect balance. "Really, don't worry about it. I understand."

"You know, I think you're the first woman I've been out with that could actually understand that."

I smiled again and then nodded as he started talking about his work. The first woman? No, probably not. But maybe I was the first woman that he thought could possibly understand him at all. I didn't know what that said about him or me. And I was getting that weird sensation in my stomach that said I was probably making a mistake by staying out on this date. However, Jason was a nice guy, and I wasn't going to just walk out when things got uncomfortable. I needed to persevere. Break the ice. Take one for the team so I could figure out exactly what I wanted to do.

"So, I was thinking of having the lamb tonight. What about you?"

The idea of eating anything that was a baby animal really wasn't my favorite, but I wasn't going to say anything. Maybe I would go vegetarian tonight.

"There's that portobello ravioli that sounds amazing. The one in the cream sauce?"

"Ah, that sounds good, too. Though I don't know if I

could do pasta right now." He patted what was most likely his washboard abs and grinned. And then he winked.

Was winking a thing? Did people still wink? Of course, they did. I had guy friends that winked. But why did this one feel weird?

"Well, I'm going for the pasta."

"And the heavy cream," he said, winking again.

Was I being fat-shamed? Or eating-shamed. Because, no, I wasn't the most slender woman in the world. I had curves, and I liked them. Moyer had liked them, too, thank you very much.

I had lost about twenty-five pounds after losing Moyer. Mostly because I couldn't stomach anything. I had gained it all back recently, though, and it had gone straight to my hips and my boobs. And, yes, the little pouch on my stomach, but whatever. I was perfectly healthy, and if I wanted pasta and cream sauce, I was going to have the damn pasta and cream sauce.

I let out a breath, still keeping the smile that my mother had taught me.

"Well, it's a treat." It wasn't a treat. It was pasta. I ate in moderation. And now I was judging myself, and I did not like it.

Enough.

"Well, maybe we'll just have to skip dessert, or at least dessert here." He winked again.

Why did I hate winking? And why did I hate the innuendo that said he thought he was actually going to sleep with me tonight?

And as that thought sent bile straight to my throat, I sipped my wine, giving him a not-so-pleasant smile. I knew it didn't reach my eyes this time, but then again, Jason didn't really catch that, did he?

Oh, I really shouldn't have gone out on this date.

Because while sitting across from another man while eating dinner was one thing, the idea of actually sleeping with someone else? So not there.

Yes, I'd had dreams about sleeping with three of the four Chrises, but that did not actually mean I was ready to sleep with someone. I could barely stomach the idea of the dreams with Chris Hemsworth, Chris Evans, and Chris Pine. Together. Sometimes, Chris Pang would show up, as well.

I let my mind drift, thinking about that dream and exactly how I'd woken up.

Jason was giving me a weird look, and I figured I should probably stop thinking about that particular Chris dream period. I would save it for later. When I was alone. Because after this dinner? I was definitely going to be alone. There was no way I was going on a second date with Jason.

Regardless of how perfect his teeth and jaw were.

We ordered our food and talked pleasantries about the weather and our favorite TV shows.

We talked about families, and how our parents and grandparents knew each other from the country club. I just nodded. I figured if he wanted to talk about the country club set, he would probably mention this date to his parents or his grandparents and then those people would speak to my family. And I really did not want to deal with that. I loved my family. Seriously adored them. But, sometimes, they were just a little too much for me. Hence why I worked at a nonprofit and hung out at a bar downtown with my friends rather than at the country club where Jason apparently spent most of his time.

We finished our food, and I declined an offer to taste the lamb. He, however, did not decline to try my pasta.

Well, who was eating pasta and cream sauce now? Huh, Jason?

We were just about to order dessert, or at least he was because I wasn't about to touch dessert right then, when his phone buzzed again, and he cursed.

My brows rose, not at the curse but the way he said it. I cursed all the time, but he had very pleasantly not done so. As if this were maybe a façade. Or perhaps I was just looking too much into it.

"Is there something wrong?"

He shook his head and then nodded. Well, that wasn't confusing at all.

"I hate to do this, but I have to go."

I blinked. "Oh?" This couldn't be one of those emergency calls or texts, could it? The same type my friend Violet had sent to me earlier to see if I needed to get out of the date? Emergency calls didn't usually come after dinner had been served.

"Yeah, something with work." He cleared his throat and wiped his mouth with his linen napkin. "I'll leave some cash on the table for my half, and we'll call it a day?"

Oh. This was one of those dates.

"You know, the whole women's liberation thing. Don't want you to feel like I have to take care of you or anything." And then he winked. Again. I officially hated winking.

"It's no problem, Jason." I smiled, knowing it surely didn't reach my eyes this time. And then I patted the side of the table as if I were patting the check that hadn't arrived. "How about I take care of this one?"

"That sounds great." He grinned, pulling on his coat. "Maybe I'll take care of the next one?"

I didn't say anything, I just smiled.

He leaned over, kissed my cheek, and then was off doing a job I didn't actually know anything about.

I blinked and then carefully took my linen napkin and wiped my cheek.

Well. Looked like I just paid for a very expensive dinner at a place that wasn't my favorite, but at least the date was over. Thank God.

The waitress came, frowning just slightly before she gave me that placid smile again.

"Is there anything else I can get you?" I knew there were more questions in those eyes of hers, but she didn't ask them. This was a nice place, after all.

"I would love a cup of tea. Do you mind taking the plates away?"

"Of course, miss." She named off a few tea types, and I ordered the chamomile, needing something to settle my nerves. It was either that or a shot of whiskey.

I sat alone at the table, something I was definitely used to. After Moyer, I had learned how to eat alone at restaurants. Learned how to ignore the curious looks of people wondering why I was alone and not with another person. It didn't bother me anymore, and oddly enough, being left in the middle of a date really didn't bother me either.

"Harmony?"

I had just taken a sip of my newly arrived tea when I heard his voice.

His.

Brendon.

"Brendon?"

"Hey, there. I was heading to the bar to eat rather than at a table since it's busy tonight."

He smiled at me. This time, I smiled back.

Brendon was my friend, and he didn't wink unless something was actually funny.

"Well, why don't you join me?" I said, gesturing towards the other side of the table.

He frowned and looked over his shoulder. "Are you sure? Are you waiting for someone?"

I shook my head. "Oh, I'm sure you'll hear about it eventually, but my date is officially over."

Something flashed across his eyes, and I wondered what it was.

"Do I need to hurt someone for you?"

That made me laugh. "No, but why don't you eat something, and maybe I'll get some dessert." *With extra whipped cream*, though I didn't say that.

"Are you sure?"

I nodded. "Don't sit at the bar, share my table. Okay?"

He sat down, and the waitress whisked away Jason's water glass and put down a glass for Brendon. He quickly ordered what he wanted, having apparently memorized the menu much like I had, and soon we were sitting there, me drinking tea, him drinking a glass of red wine, and both of us just talking.

When I looked at Brendon, I couldn't help but think of Moyer, but not in the way most people might think.

You know that part of the movie *Practical Magic* when you're screaming at the husband to move out of the way because you know what's coming since the curse hadn't been broken? When you're so worried about the bikes that you don't see the truck coming?

I felt as though I lived through that, even though I wasn't there and I'm not a witch.

Brendon was there, though.

He and Moyer worked together for a few years after they got out of college, and they had become good friends. They'd gone out to lunch to meet me since I could spare the time from work and were running late.

So, it was Brendon who stood on the corner and watched my husband die.

Witnesses would tell my family, who would later tell me, that Brendon had reached out for Moyer. He'd called his name as if trying to will my husband not to take that final step.

But Moyer hadn't heard. No, he had been too focused on answering my call rather than listening to his friend as he called out to him. Moyer hadn't chosen to listen, or maybe he just hadn't had the time. He hadn't heard.

After all, the split-second decisions where one could make the wrong choice or the right one was out of our hands when the true things mattered. The ones where there isn't a choice at all.

The driver of the delivery truck hadn't seen the red light. He hadn't seen my husband in the crosswalk. He hadn't been tired, hadn't been drunk, but he had been confused in the series of one-way streets as he got delayed in his delivery.

He'd missed the light changing from green to yellow to red at the precise wrong moment.

And Brendon had looked at his shoe—at least that's what the others told me later. He'd looked down because he had stepped in gum or something, and he'd hesitated for a brief moment before going out to the crosswalk.

The one that had signaled them to move. My husband had moved. He had walked. There was no countdown, no red hand telling him to stop. Instead, there was a man in white, telling him to go.

And I had called at the precise right moment...or was it the wrong one?

I hadn't heard my husband die. The phone had connected, but I hadn't heard him say hello. He hadn't heard me say hello either. All I knew was that the call connected quickly, and then nothing. There were no sirens, no sounds of the truck. There were no traffic sounds or screaming.

And like in *Practical Magic*, I wasn't there.

Nor was I searching for the black beetle.

My husband had died because of an accident. In a quick—hopefully painless—way. At least, that's what the doctors told me.

Brendon had been the one to see it all. And it had changed everything. Not just for me, but also for him. Months passed where I didn't speak to Brendon. He'd been Moyer's friend, and mine too in a way. But we had drifted. And maybe that was for a reason.

Maybe it was because of him.

Maybe it was because of me.

Maybe Brendon saw Moyer when he looked at me. I didn't know. After all, when my guards were down like they were tonight, I saw my husband in Brendon, as well.

We'd drifted so far apart that seeing him now was a bit jarring, but it shouldn't have been. When our friend Allison died, the Connolly brothers came back into my life. Just as they were brought back into the lives of my friends.

But now Brendon was here in front of me, and there were no ghosts in the room.

Only in my heart.

And maybe his.

CHAPTER TWO

BRENDON

I RAN FROM THE SOUND, but my legs weren't moving fast enough. It was like no matter what I did, something kept pulling me back, screaming at me. Yet it was a whisper at the same time. I tried to shout, attempted to call for help, but it was like my mouth was full of wet paper.

I froze where I was, even though I knew I should run, and tried to pull the obstruction out, but it just kept coming back, as if my mouth, my throat, and my lungs were full of it.

I couldn't breathe, couldn't find a way to not have whatever it was in my mouth.

I couldn't call for help, couldn't do anything.

And then, suddenly, I could taste again, I could breathe. So I moved my feet, only I couldn't keep them on the ground, it was like I was floating in midair just slightly, enough so I couldn't move forward but I also wasn't moving up.

I was just in stasis, floating as if I were waiting for something.

The darkness came, and I could feel its spindly claws wrapping around my ankle, pulling me closer to it. It whispered my name, a soft caress that went straight to my heart, twisting it into pulp. Tears ran down my face, and I tried to call out again, but there were no words, was no breath.

I kicked out and was somehow able to lift a little higher away from the darkness. I tried to move my arms and my legs. I didn't know how to fly. But I knew how to swim. Maybe if I could just breaststroke through the air as if I were underwater, I could get away from the darkness.

But it kept coming after me.

It kept screaming my name, screaming so loudly that it filled my ears and ended in a whisper. An echo.

"Brendon."

A scrape of nails.

"Brendon."

A breath of air on the back of my neck.

And then it was above me, waiting. It touched my neck, and I screamed.

I opened my eyes, and I knew that I was finally awake. I wiped my brow, sweat coating my skin as I let out a sigh.

One day, I would stop having these dreams, but considering that I was almost thirty, I figured it wouldn't be anytime soon. It wasn't even like they were full anxiety dreams. Those always stressed me out.

When I was away from the bar, from my family, I'd always had dreams where I couldn't wait tables fast enough or couldn't get enough beer into glasses for all of my foster father's customers.

It was like I was suddenly right back in my old place, and everyone was saying that I had missed a shift but that I still had to work for the rest of the week. Or I was back in school or college and I hadn't turned in a paper, even though I'd thought I finished everything on time. Then there were those anxiety dreams where I had apparently missed a class for the whole semester and had to take a final that I wasn't prepared for.

All of those stress dreams were something I was used to. Something I could wake up from and wonder why I was so stressed out. But these dreams weren't anxiety dreams. It was like they were memories. Memories of a time I'd rather forget. But, apparently, my mind was never going to let me forget exactly what had happened when I was younger.

The time before Jack, before Rose, before I met my brothers and found a family.

No, those dreams would just keep creeping in on me until I felt as if I had nothing left to give, nothing left to take.

I turned over and looked at my phone, squinting at the glare. Apparently, during an update, I had taken off the filter that usually helps with the brightness. I cursed myself. It was four-thirty in the morning. Too late for anything to be really happening, and too early for me to be up.

But there was no way I could go back to sleep. At least it wasn't three-thirty like it usually was. For some reason, between three and three-thirty in the morning was when I normally had my nightmares. As if that were the time when I knew I should be awake and annoyed with myself. It was around that time that I could usually last about an hour, tossing and turning, maybe even getting up to go pee. But at four-thirty? Considering that my alarm would go off in about an hour, I didn't really know if I had that in me. I turned on my side again and frowned. Maybe I should just get up. I knew I had enough work to do. I was working two jobs, even though I had told myself I would only stick to one. But, apparently, old me hadn't changed.

21

At least not enough.

When I was in high school, I had worked two jobs. At Jack and Rose's bar, and at a restaurant down the street. I had wanted to save money for college even though Jack and Rose had said they would cover it. It was hard to rely on people, even the ones who were the best people in the entire world.

Even those who had never once failed me or let me down.

I'd needed a backup plan.

I had needed a way to escape just in case I couldn't rely on anyone.

It didn't matter that I loved Jack and Rose. That they were my parents. They had adopted me, just like they'd taken in Cameron and Aiden. I loved my family, but I was so afraid that everything was going to fall apart again that I always had one foot out the door.

Maybe they had known that. Perhaps that's why they'd held me so close and didn't give me space. Maybe that was why it was so easy to walk away when Cameron did.

I pinched the bridge of my nose, remembering that time, recalling the fact that my go-bag was still in my closet.

I let out a rough breath. I was almost thirty years old, and I still had a go-bag packed just in case I had to leave.

Nothing was chasing me, no one was coming after me anymore. I had no ties to the places I used to live before Jack and Rose found me. No connections to the world that had tried to beat me down and take everything from me.

The world that *had* beaten me down and taken too much from me.

When I lived in Jack and Rose's house before I moved out to go to college, I'd always had a go-bag. One that was filled with clothes, money, things I could use on the road, while on the run.

I wasn't an international thief or someone who actually needed a go-bag, but when I was injured, I had put everything I had into a bag and held it close to me. I'd slept with it when I was on the streets, even when I had been in different foster homes before I landed on Jack and Rose's doorstep.

Hell, I had slept with it for far longer than I cared to admit when I was in their house. Aiden and Cameron never once made fun of me for it. They had their own issues, and they just looked at me and shrugged and then went about their business. It really wasn't until I put that go-bag in the closet rather than in my bed that I felt like maybe there could be a connection between the twins and me.

And I still had a go-bag in my closet. It just kept me

safe, helped me with my anxiety. Although with the dreams I'd been having lately, maybe my anxiety was still a little off the charts.

But I couldn't really help it. Between my job and saving Jack's bar, I sort of felt like I was burning the candle at both ends.

It also didn't help that my family was finally starting to come back together after we had fallen apart.

I looked over at the clock and realized that twenty minutes had passed. I didn't think that I was going back to sleep. It seemed that today would be at least a four-cup coffee day. Usually, I could last on two—sometimes three. But today? Totally four. Maybe even five if I lived dangerously.

I slid out of bed and turned off my alarm. Then I went to pee and brush my teeth and take a shower. I would have to take another one later, but I really wanted to wash off the cold sweat that had added a filmy layer to my skin thanks to the nightmare.

I hadn't had that particular nightmare in a while, the one that sort of mixed everything together. I wasn't really happy about it.

I had no idea what had triggered it, other than the fact that, apparently, there was a fourth Connolly brother.

I let the lukewarm water slide over me, not wanting to

go too hot or too cold this morning since my skin felt a little irritated from the dream.

When Cameron had left us to go see his birth mom, it had created a rift in the family.

He'd still talked to my parents, mostly because he couldn't really *not* talk to Jack and Rose. They were family. But he had broken ties with both Aiden and me because we hadn't been there when he needed us. Aiden had felt betrayed or some shit because he assumed that Cameron had chosen their mom over him, the same woman who'd left them behind and preferred drugs and men over her children. And so, I had stayed behind too. Hadn't answered Cameron's calls for a while because I was on Aiden's side. I had thought my brother left me, too.

My go-bag had been filled to the brim at that point, even though we were out of college and starting our lives in the adult world of jobs and mortgages.

But now Dillon was here, Cameron was back, and we were a family again. Rose had died a few years ago, and Cameron had come home for the funeral, but he hadn't brought Dillon then. He hadn't even really spoken to us, just grieved with Jack and then left. I hadn't understood it then, but Cameron had been dealing with his own hell when it came to Dillon and trying to raise him after finally losing their mother when she overdosed.

And then Cameron had come back when Jack died, and the bar had been left to the three of us.

But this time, Cam decided to move permanently, dragging an eighteen-year-old Dillon with him.

Things had been rocky at first, with the bar failing and our family failing even worse, but now the bar was doing well, and I had a feeling as long as we kept up with what we needed to do, it would do just fine in the future, too.

It was a legacy, and we were all determined to keep it that way.

Things were still a little tense with the four of us, but we were doing well. I liked Dillon. He was a good kid if a little too lazy sometimes—as all teens finding themselves were. But he had a good heart, and I thought he would do well. He was going to college in the spring and was even thinking about going to culinary school, following in his brother Aiden's footsteps.

My plan was to just stand there and try to help, watch it all as a passive observer who wasn't so passive. I got out of the shower and wrapped a towel around my waist, wondering why I was so introspective today.

That dream had put so much weird energy into me that I needed to run it out. So, I towel-dried my hair and put on my jogging gear, knowing that it would be a little too fucking cold to do this. But maybe the briskness would help.

I put a hat over my still-wet hair and bundled up before stretching and starting my exercise. I jogged when I had too much energy, and I ran so I could keep up with myself, with everything that kept coming up around me. I wasn't the most athletic person and was probably even less athletic than Cameron and Aiden, but I tried. I was a little more slender than my brothers and worked hard to stay disciplined.

Plus, I was planning to run a 10K with my friend Harmony soon. She was training, and that meant I would be training, as well. She hadn't wanted to do it alone, and none of the rest of her friends were really interested in running for sport.

The cold air slapped my face, and I shivered as I kept my pace. I pushed thoughts of that 10K out of my mind and exactly who I'd be running with because I didn't have time for that train of thought at all. Plus, the idea of jogging and running that long really didn't appeal to me, but I was doing it because Harmony needed me.

And I would do anything for her.

And that's enough of that.

I kept up my brisk pace, waiting for the sun to come up even though it wouldn't for at least another hour. We were too far into the winter for that to happen, so now I would just be running in the dark like a crazy person.

But considering that I used to live on these streets, it

didn't really bother me. I already had enough nightmares, I might as well run through the safely-lit places and try to forget the time before when I didn't have a home, where I was dirty, and everything just kept coming at me.

I swallowed hard, annoyed with myself. My breathing was smooth, my pace decent, and yet I couldn't stop thinking about everything that was happening around me. I couldn't stop thinking about the past and what the future might hold.

I already had too much on my plate, yet I knew I would just continue to add to it so I didn't have to think about what was important.

Like the fact that I missed Jack and Rose as if I had lost a limb. They'd taken me in, were my first real family. And now they were gone, and they'd left behind the shambles of what our family once was.

I knew it wasn't their fault that my brothers and I had broken apart, that we had failed each other. Jack and Rose had done their best to mend the rift, but it hadn't been enough because our ghosts were stronger.

But now the three of us—four of us, actually—were better than we used to be. We had needed time to grow apart so we could come together stronger.

I just wished that Jack and Rose were alive to witness it.

There was a lot of stupid decisions made on all of our

parts, and I hated that Rose and Jack ever thought that what happened was their fault.

They were the good in the bad of the world and, honestly, they had deserved far better than us.

I finished my jog and went back into my house, taking another shower. I sometimes took upwards of three a day. I knew my water bill was astronomical, and it wasn't the best thing for the environment or my body, but I couldn't help it.

I needed to be clean.

For a man who didn't know when he would get his next shower, when the idea of the dirt caked onto my skin meant another layer of warmth, it was the best thing for me.

I needed to stay clean, and my clothes had to be meticulous. I practically paid a living wage to the dry cleaners.

I got out of the shower, did my hair, dealt with everything else, and tried not to fall asleep since I needed more coffee. Then I slid into my suit, the crispness feeling like a second skin.

It was clean, *I* was clean, something I desperately needed. After living for so long in filth, I had a tendency to overdo the cleanliness. I looked at myself in the mirror, pulled back my dark hair again, and nodded.

"This'd better be good enough," I said to myself.

Then I went to work.

Because that's what I did.

I worked two jobs. One was helping with the bar. Jack and Rose had left the place to the three of us, and I was in charge of the business side and bringing more people in with different, innovative ideas. It wasn't easy, and it wasn't my forte, but with Aiden in the kitchen, and Cameron as the face of the company, we were doing pretty damn well.

We had some good staff, including Dillon as a busboy and waiter, and Beckham was a pretty damn good bartender. We would be okay.

It had been a little sticky at first, but between the pool tournament and Aiden's food, and the different beers that Cameron was bringing in, we were getting a better clientele. A deeper one.

But before I could do any of that, I had to go to my other job. The one I had started with.

My career was to buy and sell businesses. To make them better and more efficient. It was much like I was doing with Jack's old bar, the Connolly Brewery, but on a far grander scale. I never explained what I did to others because it confused them. While it made me a lot of money, it was also a ton of work. And considering that a large percentage of my earnings went to the different shelters around the city, it meant that I had to work twice as hard to make sure that I didn't end up on the streets again.

I went to my office and nodded at my executive assistant who was already typing away.

She was older than me by a good twenty years and had far more experience than I could ever hope for, for someone in her position. I had offered her a job in sales, and she had simply shaken her head, saying that she liked where she was. She enjoyed bossing us around rather than having to be the boss.

I'd just smiled and doubled her salary.

Fran was the reason our company worked, and she should be paid for that.

I looked over at the empty office and frowned. I had offered her the place where Moyer used to work. The office that was still empty most days. When Moyer died, the company had taken a hit. Not financially, but emotionally.

Moyer had been part of sales, and an integral cog in our machine.

The person that had taken his position usually worked remotely because she was a mother of three, and it was easier for all of us if she stayed home a lot of the time to help with her kids.

It didn't bother me at all. I had even offered to put in a daycare center at the company itself, and maybe that would come one day. But for now, she telecommuted well.

And that meant that Moyer's office stood empty most of the time.

Yes, she worked there sometimes. And, yes, it was still her office, but it would always be Moyer's in my mind.

And when I thought about Moyer, I thought about Harmony.

I shook my head and sat down at my desk, booting up my computer so I could start work.

I had meeting after meeting, a couple of phone conferences, and then some more admin work to get done before I could hand things off to Fran and others and get to the bar. But I kept thinking about dinner the night before and how I had just wanted some peace and quiet and ended up eating dinner while Harmony drank tea and had dessert, both of us laughing.

She'd made me laugh. I didn't do it often, not because I was sad or angry with the world, but because I was a little more contemplative than others. And I was fine with that. I had seen enough therapists in my life to figure out exactly why that was.

But Harmony made me laugh. She made me remember the times when everything was a little lighter, when all of us had been slightly damaged but still came together as friends.

It had been the four girls and us three guys.

Me, Aiden, Cameron, Harmony, Violet, Sienna, and Allison.

We had split apart after Cameron left, each of us going our separate ways, although the girls had become an even closer unit.

Then Allison had died, and we'd all come together again. We all had different sets of friendships. I had become friends with Harmony over time because her husband had worked here. Moyer had been my friend, and Harmony had been my friend. Then we'd lost Moyer, and I tried to stay close to Harmony, tried to help, but it was too painful. For multiple reasons.

Then, everything had come together again after Allison's funeral, and we were all a little tighter now.

We weren't the same people we were before, but then again, who was? We all had different connections, different layers of relationships, and we were even adding more people to our group with Beckham and Meadow hanging out with us sometimes, and Dillon always there because he was our brother.

But it was different.

As I looked down at my computer, knowing I had work to do but my brain not in it, I knew that sometimes different wasn't good. Sometimes, different hurt and peeled you apart until you couldn't breathe.

The fragments of my dream slid into me again, and I

shook them off. I wasn't the same Brendon I had been when I lived on the streets, when I was scared at every twist and turn. But I knew that if I weren't careful, I'd break again.

Because everybody counted on me. And I had to be the strong one. Aiden and Cameron could get angry and yell at each other and just let it out. But I had to be strong.

I couldn't let any feelings that I might have break me.

Because, in the end, I wouldn't be the only one broken.

In the end, I'd be the one who shattered the others.

CHAPTER THREE

I picked out a new dress today. I have no idea if you'd have liked it. But I'd like to think you would have smiled.

- Harmony to Moyer. 3 months ATE.

HARMONY

I'D ALWAYS WRITTEN in journals. They kept me sane even when I didn't really think myself on the correct mental path at all. The day after I'd said goodbye to

Moyer, I didn't write, but I did look at a notebook, wondering if it would be prudent to write.

The day my mother had left after the funeral was the day it'd truly felt real, and that was the day I'd picked up my journal.

For every day he was gone, I wrote to him as if he could read it. Maybe he could, or perhaps I was just writing to myself because the idea of saying these things aloud was far too hard. The stuff I wrote about might not make sense to anyone else, but it did to me. It might be too personal for people to read, or too boring for anyone to care.

But they were the little moments I missed.

The times that told me I was alive.

And Moyer wasn't.

Some moments didn't make it into the journal. And maybe those were the hardest. Like the first time my period was supposed to arrive about a week after the funeral. I was late by four days when I was usually regular. I'd had no idea what to do, what to feel, so I'd taken a pregnancy test, not knowing what I hoped for. Did I want a baby? Did I want that memory? That gift? Would it hurt?

I'd peed on a stick and hadn't felt a single thing. Numbness had taken over as I tried not to think about the results.

I couldn't feel much those days.

It had been negative.

I'd felt nothing, and yet at the same time, the grief had hit again. Because, apparently, that choice had been taken from me. Then I'd bled the next day, and I'd known that the last chance for me to carry Moyer's child had been taken from me.

I'd spent the first months figuring out how to be on my own because people kept making sure I could do it, and they didn't know how to help me any other way. They'd brought in food and flowers. Had bought me blankets and pillows to keep me warm and comforted. They'd helped me with the to-do list we'd gathered from the internet and friends who'd been through similar situations. It had been odd to think that there was a checklist for becoming a widow, but apparently, it even came in your choice of template, color, and symbol.

Then, somehow, I had to be the unselfish one and let the grief in. Because it wasn't just about me. It never had been, but I'd spent so many days trying to figure out how to live, that it let me not think about the fact that Moyer was gone. Though, in the end, it wasn't as if I could forget that.

I had to let myself feel the loss. Because the *man* wasn't back. The man I loved wasn't back.

But he wasn't just the man I loved.

He was a person. And he wasn't there anymore.

There would be no smiles. No times when he'd put on his coat and grin at me. There would be no more texting him images of random, happy things.

He wouldn't get to see who won the next election or see who died on *The Walking Dead*. He'd never know what happened to our neighbor with the plants that kept dying in the front yard.

And I'd had to figure out how to make it work.

How to make my life work...

I wasn't sure I could at first. Even with my friends and family supporting me, the task had seemed insurmountable.

The funeral was the easy part. The funeral home had had a checklist. An easily useable folder with paper cut down just to the right length so you could see each of the headings without having to page through. They'd dealt in death enough that they had a template.

That was the easy part.

The hard part came later.

When the house was quiet. Because soon, people went back to their own normal while I tried to figure out my new one. They left after giving me big hugs, saying I was so strong, and then I was left alone in the house, wondering what had just happened.

And even then, that wasn't the hardest part.

That was realizing that I was now one person, not half of a whole.

The hardest part came when I had to make a menu or think about how to cook for one.

It was when I realized that I didn't want to do Christmas or Hanukkah with family members, but I didn't know how to say no.

The hardest part was deciding how to put up a tree. Deciding if I should.

It was trying to remember a password.

The hardest part was changing a lightbulb in a fixture for the first time and realizing I had no idea how to do it because it was on *his* list. Not mine.

It was having no one to hold the ladder when I needed to change that lightbulb.

The hardest part came when I had to live.

Because in the end, he couldn't.

So I had to.

And I have. For two years, I have lived.

I became a widow at the age of twenty-five, yet I felt so much older. As if I'd lived a thousand lives while Moyer only got to live a part of one.

I set down my pen and stared at the blank pages, wondering what I could say today. I didn't write to Moyer daily anymore, and for that I was grateful. I didn't wallow in death and what my life used to be, but I did write to him occasionally. He was always there in the back of my mind, or just around, as if I could feel him near.

I missed him with every breath in my soul, and yet I knew I wasn't the same Harmony I was when we were Moyer and Harmony, two young kids who'd gotten married because they loved each other and thought they had their whole future in front of them.

I shook my head and put the journal away. I'd write more later, just not today. Or maybe I wouldn't write again. It had been a couple of months since I had, and it felt like I was reaching the next level of my new normal, the one where I didn't need to journal like I had.

It wasn't an anniversary or anything, but for some reason, it felt like it was going to be a hard day. So, I'd go for a jog, something I didn't particularly like but needed to do to train for the 10k I was planning, and then I'd eat something with a lot of carbs that wasn't good for me.

I'd learned to let go of those insecurities when everything else fell apart. Sometimes, after running a few miles to train, I totally deserved a glazed donut.

I put everything away and stood up, stretching. I needed to change into my workout gear, even though part of me really just wanted to curl up on the couch with a book and not do anything.

But because I knew that wasn't good for me, at least right now, I changed into my workout gear and continued my stretching because I knew it wasn't going to be easy today. My body hurt, and my heart ached a little, too.

Maybe that date had annoyed me more than I thought.

I'd always thought that going on my first date after Moyer would be easy. But feeling slightly dejected afterwards? No, I wasn't a fan of that. I had thought maybe if I were dejected at all, it would be because of my feelings for Moyer and how he would possibly feel as though I was cheating on him. But that hadn't come up at all. Instead, I just hadn't felt any connection with Jason, even though I probably should have.

He was nice, if a little self-centered, maybe a little egocentric, but perhaps I was only glimpsing the surface. Maybe he had more depth.

And then I remembered him making a casual comment about the pasta that I wanted to eat and the fact that he had assumed we were going to split the check because of the women's movement and all that.

No, I would not be going on a date with Jason again. And, no, it had nothing to do—or at least mostly nothing to do—with the lack of chemistry.

No, that was all Jason.

I shook those thoughts from my mind, zipped myself up in my thick jogging jacket considering it was a bit chilly outside, and made sure that my earphones were all set so I could listen to my book or music, depending on what I needed.

Sometimes, I needed loud music so I couldn't hear my feet hit the ground. It helped to put myself back in my mind so I wasn't actually thinking about jogging and the fact that I didn't really appreciate or like it. But, sometimes, I needed a book so I could just be lost in that, and it didn't matter that I could hear my feet hitting the ground.

I was weird, but I accepted that.

I stretched one more time but not overmuch so I wouldn't hurt myself, and then started my jog.

I had been part of the cross-country team in high school, though I had been in the middle of the pack—never a ribbon winner, and never at the end. I liked feeling that way, like no one could really see what I was doing and didn't pay too much attention. That let me just be myself rather than the person other people thought I needed to be.

I slowed my breathing, trying to calm myself as I worked up a sweat even in the frigid air.

Even when I was younger, I'd had responsibilities. I was the daughter of well-to-do parents, and I went to school with lots of well-to-do children. It didn't matter that it was a public school, it was in a very nice neighborhood where everybody knew each other's families. Or at least it had felt that way sometimes. I had to be the perfect daughter, the perfect student, and the perfect human. Never a stray hair out of place.

So, being able to hide in the middle of the pack when it came to jogging and cross-country had been helpful. My parents hadn't pushed me for more because they did so in all other aspects. And though they were loving and caring, they had pushed a little too hard sometimes.

They ended up apologizing to me later for that, and I had taken that with grace. Considering I'd gone through so much else in my life, having parents who only wanted the best for their child didn't seem like too bad of a thing.

They'd stood by my side when I lost Moyer, and they'd helped me in every way possible. In fact, in some ways, we were closer now than we had been when I was growing up.

We were definitely closer than we had been when I was a married wife in my own home, living my own life. Because, sometimes, when you grow up, you drift away from your parents because you have your own life and they have their own lives, as well. We'd talked weekly at that time, but now, we spoke daily.

If they didn't hear from me on any given day, they would video call the next morning, worried looks in their eyes. But I just took it all in stride, knowing that I needed that as much as they did. I talked with Violet and Sienna every day, as well. They were my best friends. And when Allison was alive, I had spoken to her just as often.

I rubbed my chest, the ever-present ache making itself known.

It made me sad to realize that I hadn't seen the pain in Allison's speeches. I hadn't noticed it. Maybe I was too focused on my own pain, my loss.

I hadn't seen that Allison was hurting, as well.

And now she was gone, and there was nothing I could do to take back those moments. To look deeper into what I might have missed.

But I had my family, I had my friends, and I even had the Connolly brothers. Three men—no, four if I included Dillon—that were always in my life now. We had come together after Allison's funeral, and I was happy that I had more people in my circle. That I wasn't exactly alone anymore.

I finished my five miles, my legs a little shaky, and my skin far too cold.

I had worn a scarf around the lower half of my face, but it didn't seem to help.

Everything was just too cold outside. Now, I just wanted some hot coffee, and then I could get back to work.

I went home, showered, and got ready for my day.

I had a few meetings later in the afternoon, and while

I could have worked from home and done everything I would have done at the office via phone, sometimes I just needed to change the setting.

But first, I needed coffee. All the coffee.

So, I drove to my favorite shop, one that still served coffee in actual mugs where I could take a seat by the fire and enjoy just ten or fifteen minutes of pure bliss with my caffeine before I had to tackle the rest of my day.

The place was all wooden accents and soft lines and was just perfect for relaxing or getting ready for the start of the day.

During the late afternoon, it would get busier with people doing their homework and other jobs on their computers, but right after the early morning rush, it was the perfect time.

The people who came in for his or her to-go cups were already at their jobs, and I was just a little bit later. I didn't mind that because it meant my favorite seat by the fire was open.

However, the seat next to mine was full. When my eyes met his, I just laughed.

"Okay, now I think you're just stalking me," I told Brendon as I unwrapped my scarf from around my neck.

Brendon got up and gave me a hug, and I leaned into his hold, inhaling his very masculine scent. Brendon always smelled nice—clean with just a little bit of an earthy undertone.

And he gave great hugs.

He'd been very careful with me after Moyer died, as if he were unsure whether he was allowed to even touch me while I was grieving. We had stopped that nervousness soon after when I fell into his arms, just needing a big hug. And Brendon had been giving me his signature hugs ever since we reconnected after the funeral.

"Yes, I'm stalking you. I'm not doing a very good job of hiding that though, am I?" Brendon said, his eyes twinkling.

"Well, this is one of the best places in Denver, so I guess we can't really complain too much."

"You want me to get you something?"

I shook my head and set my purse down on the chair. "No, you already have your coffee. Let me just go get mine. As long as you watch my purse?"

"I can do that."

"Well, thank you."

I smiled at him again and then went off in search of my caffeine. By the time I got my mug full of my favorite white mocha, I was warm again, and ready to sip slowly.

"That smells amazing," Brendon said, looking down at his black coffee. "I think I need to do better at this whole flavor thing."

I grinned. "I don't do this every day. But I just ran for a very long time in very cold weather, and I deserve this." I took a sip and let out a moan.

I didn't realize I'd actually moaned as loudly as I did until I looked up at Brendon, who was now staring at me, his eyes slightly dark. I couldn't really read the look in them, but I could feel my cheeks reddening.

"Good, is it?"

I nodded, blushing again. "Apparently, a little too good. Sorry about that."

"Don't be sorry. Maybe the next time I drink coffee, I'll get that."

I imagined Brendon moaning over his coffee and blinked. "White mochas are the best. Unless it's a caramel latte. Or a caramel macchiato. Or chai. Or just anything. Oh, I love caffeine."

Brendon smiled. "I don't think I could do what I do without caffeine." He looked at his phone and frowned. "In fact, I need to head into the office soon, but I'm getting a late start since I stayed too late there yesterday."

"I was wondering why you were here after the morning rush. I don't usually ever see you here."

Brendon took a sip of his coffee and nodded. "I'm trying not to overwork myself. And that means I get to go in a little bit later today. Plus, I get to leave early since I'm ahead on my accounts, and I'm going to knock on wood as

I say that." He literally knocked on wood just then. "But I'll probably bring my work into my other job."

I shook my head before setting my mug down. "I cannot believe you're doing both. It's a little insane, Brendon."

"I know. I'm not working as many hours as I used to, at least at the first job. I'm actually delegating and helping people do what they need to do so they can maybe own their own businesses one day like I do. You know how it is at the job, sometimes you just get a little too lost in it."

He winced, but I just shook my head. "You don't have to tiptoe around the fact that I know exactly what goes on at your business. Or the fact that Moyer used to work there, and I know the ins and outs of it. Or at least I *knew* the ins and outs of it three years ago. It's probably changed a lot since then. Businesses tend to do that."

"Sometimes I forget exactly how to speak to you without stepping on my own feet."

"You're doing just fine, Brendon. I mean, we've had a few months now to get used to this new dynamic of ours. The one where we're friends in a group rather than Moyer's friend and Moyer's wife."

"That is true, though I knew you before you met Moyer," he said softly.

"I know. So that means that you can just be yourself around me even more. It's sort of what we do. Or at least what we should. Anyway, we are the best pool players in the area, so we need to unite against the others."

Brendon laughed at that, and I shook my head. When the Connollys' brewery was in trouble just a few months ago, they had opened up a pool league to get new people in. It had worked, but it had taken all of us to get it there. I had partnered with Brendon since we knew each other the best, and somehow, we ended up winning the entire thing. I had given my money back to the brewery rather than taking it for myself, though Brendon had been a little annoyed about that. But considering that he had done the same thing, he couldn't really say much. I had money, and I didn't need any more than I had. I just wanted to make sure that the Connolly brothers' business did well, and that meant giving back to it.

"I cannot believe we actually made up that dance," Brendon said, laughing.

"It was an amazing dance. Sort of. Sort of like a twenty's vibe with flossing in it? I don't really remember. I blocked it out."

Brendon just shook his head and then started talking about his brothers as I nodded along, laughing every once in a while.

We had taken about ten minutes before the end of the championship round to figure out and plan a victory dance—or at least learn one. It had been silly, a combination of moves that made no sense but made others laugh. Especially because no one would have thought that proper Harmony, and even more proper Brendon would dance like that.

It had been fun just to laugh and feel carefree. Because some days, I didn't feel that way.

Some days, it felt like I had the world on my shoulders and there was no coming back from that.

But I was getting better, I was healing.

Because I was Harmony, I wasn't the label.

And with friends like Brendon, it was easier to remember exactly what that meant.

CHAPTER FOUR

BRENDON

I KNEW I WAS DREAMING. I always knew. It didn't make it any easier to live the dream.

It was an oddly warm day, and all I really wanted to do was eat something and then maybe go to bed. Yeah, it was the middle of the workday, and it was only lunchtime, but I was exhausted. I had been working too many hours, and I really just didn't want to be here right now. I wanted to be at home, away from the office, and not working as many hours as I was.

But the business was doing well, and I was afraid that if I didn't work as hard as I had when we first started getting it up and running, it would fail. And I couldn't let that happen.

"You look like you need a drink, and we're not really at drinking time, are we?" Moyer said, coming into my office with a grin on his face.

"Oh, shut up. Afternoon beers are a thing. Or martini lunches. Right?"

"Well, I guess we can make that happen. We're meeting Harmony soon, right?" Moyer looked down at his phone, frowning. "I don't want to make her wait for us."

I stood up quickly, closing the blinds in my office, considering the sun kept beating down on me. No wonder it felt like an obscenely warm day.

"No problem. Let's head out. Although me being the third wheel at your lunch date with your wife doesn't really sound like too much fun for me."

Moyer just rolled his eyes and wrapped his arm around my shoulders, giving me a tight squeeze. Moyer was good like that, affectionate but not too much, just enough to make sure you knew you were wanted, that there was someone always in your corner.

"You're never a third wheel. Plus, I'm sure Harmony has friends who you could hook up with. Well, not hook up, because I don't want to have to deal with that drama if you dump them. But you remember Violet, Sienna, and Allison, right?"

I nodded, making sure I had my wallet and phone in my pockets as we walked out of the building. "Yes, we all know each other from school. I don't really hang out with them anymore. After all, my brothers used to date two of them. Kind of awkward."

There were other things I didn't say, but Moyer knew them. Moyer knew a lot, considering I didn't really talk with my family anymore other than my parents and sometimes Aiden every once in a while. Cameron was long gone, and it sucked, but there was nothing I could do.

"Well, I'm sure she has other friends. We can find you someone."

I rolled my eyes. "Please do not hook me up with anyone. I'm just fine on my own. In fact, I had a really nice date last week."

"Yeah, and did you actually talk with her afterwards?"

"No, because she spent the entire time talking about her ex and how much she still loved him and how this whole thing was so hard on her. I counseled her into maybe talking with him again if the only reason they broke up was because they thought they loved each other too much."

Moyer started laughing, and I shook my head, closing my eyes.

"You see? Do you see what I have to deal with? By the way, she texted me yesterday to let me know that they're back together, and she wanted to make sure that I knew that their first child would be named after me. Those are the kind of dates I go on, apparently."

Moyer kept laughing, and I frowned. "Okay, maybe I do need to get better at dating. But not all of us are as lucky as you."

Moyer grinned at me, his eyes full of happiness that I knew wasn't faked at all. "My wife? Best woman on the fucking planet. I'm one lucky man, and I know it every single day. Yeah, I know I got lucky, but there are other women out there. We can find you one. One that isn't in love with her ex. One that doesn't have such poor hygiene that she actually leaves a trail behind her."

I shuddered. "Okay, there was that one woman that had like food in her teeth all the time. She told me she had sworn off brushing because the man and technology wanted her to do so." I shuddered. "Ugh, I'm so glad I never kissed her."

"Well, if you had, I'm sure you'd still be able to taste that to this day."

I swallowed hard, trying not to throw up. "Okay, now I'm not hungry anymore. Maybe you should just go with Harmony, and I'll go find a hole to crawl into."

"No, you're coming with me, and you're going to have a really good lunch with my wife. Because she's amazing, and you guys are actually friends. You've been friends with her longer than you've been friends with me. So, the three of us are going to have a damn good meal, and then we're going to go back to work and make all the money. And then I'm going to go home and have an amazing dinner with my wife that we'll both cook because we like doing that together, and then I'm going to have some amazing sex. Because that is the kind of man I am."

I gave him a dry look. "Really? *Really?* I'm telling you about my horrible dating life, and you're just going to brag like that?"

"I can't help it. I'm a lucky man."

We stood on the edge of the street, waiting for the crosswalk to tell us to go, and I looked over at my friend, wondering what it was like to be that happy.

Moyer and Harmony had married young, sure, but they were so desperately in love that it just radiated off them.

I wasn't jealous of them, not really. I knew my time would come. And if it didn't, then I would find other things to put my soul into. I was just lucky to be where I was, considering where I'd come from.

And Moyer and Harmony were some of the best people I knew. The fact that they'd let me into their lives and didn't mind the fact that sometimes, yes, I was the third wheel, meant the world to me.

Moyer picked up his phone, looking down at it as it started to ring. From the smile on his face, I knew who it was. We were indeed running late, and I bet Harmony was making sure we were on our way.

The crosswalk light changed, telling us to go, and I took a step, only to frown when I realized I had stepped in gum. Seriously? Of all the things.

"Damn it," I cursed, and picked up my foot.

And then everything changed. And I couldn't really breathe.

I looked up and to the left, and there was a truck. One that shouldn't be there. There shouldn't be anything at all. This was the crosswalk. There was a red light. The walk light was white. This wasn't supposed to happen.

I reached out, trying to grab Moyer's shoulder to pull him back, but he had already taken an extra step.

"Moyer!"

I called out his name, but I swear it was a whisper, maybe it wasn't even real.

Then there was a sound, one I couldn't understand. There was glass, there was screaming. Was the screaming coming from me?

I couldn't breathe, I couldn't take another step, I couldn't do anything.

Instead, I just stood there as darkness swallowed me, as I watched my best friend die.

My eyes opened, and I knew that I was once again in my bedroom. The dream was just as vivid as it had been before. It was so intense that I felt like I was living it again.

I lay there, sweating, my hands shaking, my whole body cold and clammy.

Tears streamed down my face, but I didn't wipe them away. I hadn't even realized I was crying in my sleep, but then again, I did it far too often when it came to that dream.

I'd had nightmares my whole life, and I had the experiences to back them up. But it was that dream, the one that I relived far too often that sent me into a tailspin.

I could remember every single moment of that afternoon. I could remember feeling the heat of the sun on my face, seeing the crinkle at the corners of Moyer's eyes as he smiled.

I could remember the sound of the phone ringing as he picked up his cell and smiled some more.

I remembered thinking that it must be Harmony on the other line, that she was the one calling.

I remembered the smell of the diesel from the truck. Before that, I remembered the smell of bagels from the shop we passed on our way to the street.

I remembered patting my pockets to actually feel my wallet and phone.

I remembered being tired from overworking myself that day, and I remembered how tired I felt after.

In my dreams, I never got past that point. I never got to the part where I walked out to the middle of the street and tried to save my friend.

In my dreams, I didn't go and talk to the authorities, and I wasn't the one who spoke to Harmony.

I never got to those parts in my dreams.

Instead, I just witnessed the incident with the truck, over and over.

Sometimes it was on a loop, and I couldn't wake up until I screamed myself awake, my sheets on the floor, and my body rolled up into a ball as I scratched my arms and tried to wake myself up even though I couldn't.

I'd had night terrors as a kid, but these were so much different.

These weren't about what had happened to me when I was living on the streets. Instead, it was what had happened when I hadn't been fast enough. When I hadn't been able to save my friend.

Because it wasn't Moyer's fault. And if I hadn't stepped on gum, I'd have been right next to him. Maybe I'd been able to pull him back. Or perhaps I would have been in the street with him. Maybe we both would have been hit. But it didn't matter because it happened the way it did, and I was likely going to dream those dreams for the rest of my life.

I swallowed hard and forced myself into a sitting position, my gut feeling like there was a hole burned into it, and my whole body feeling as if maybe I had gotten hit by that truck instead.

I missed my friend. Most days, I could think of him and smile.

But after a dream like that? I couldn't do much but try to deal with it, deal with the adrenaline in my system and the guilt that wracked my body.

And there wasn't just the guilt that came after losing a friend, of not being fast enough.

No, there was the blame that came with the aftermath. The culpability that came with knowing that I wasn't the good man everyone thought I was. Because if I were, maybe I wouldn't have these feelings I did for the one person I shouldn't.

The woman who didn't deserve what I felt when I was near her.

I swallowed hard and then got out of bed, my whole body still shaking.

It was early, around five in the morning, so that meant I could work out again, maybe go for a jog and then start my jobs.

Because if I just kept focusing on the here and now, kept working towards a point in the future, then I wouldn't think about the fact that I missed Moyer. And I wouldn't think about the fact that I was slowly falling for his wife.

Because I was the worst sort of man. The type that coveted, even if he hadn't before everything changed.

I hadn't felt anything like I did now when Moyer was alive. Harmony had just been my friend, nothing more. I had only thought of her in a platonic way, it had never once crossed my mind to think of her as anything but that.

But now, things were changing, and I hated myself more every day for it.

It had started to shift in the months after losing Moyer, and I had distanced myself from that. Yes, I was a bastard for not staying near Harmony when she might have needed me, but I hadn't been able to stay.

And now, I didn't know what to do. And there wasn't really anything for me *to* do.

So, instead, I got out of bed, pulled off my boxer briefs and shoved them into the hamper before stripping my bed and putting the sheets in the washer. I was getting too good at this, dealing with the fact that I couldn't sleep and my body kept betraying me.

I didn't want to be good at this. I didn't want those dreams anymore. But it didn't look like I was going to get an answer. I wasn't going to have a choice.

I took a shower, washing the sweat from my body, and trying not to feel like I was doing something wrong.

I wasn't.

I knew that it wasn't my fault. I knew that the things I was feeling had nothing to do with the past.

I knew that I was doing okay, that I wasn't making mistake after mistake.

But I couldn't really help how I felt, not after those dreams. Because they just intensified everything, and it made me feel like I was making every wrong decision there was to make.

So, I just needed to work that out of my system, and then I could go about my day. I could pretend that everything was fine and that I wasn't losing my mind. It just wasn't easy when I kept having the same dream time and again.

I had a small gym in my basement, one that had taken a few dollars to make happen. I didn't always work out at the same times everyone else did, and honestly, I didn't like working out next to people. It stressed me out. I'd rather just do what I did at home. Yes, I was privileged to do so, but it was helpful, and that meant I could lift weights, box, and do some cardio without anyone looking at me.

I figured that was sort of a plus.

Considering that I hadn't had anything to my name for many years, being able to say that I had a home gym was sort of a weird thing for me. It wasn't like I told anyone else, but being able to hoard that for myself was just like the go-bag that I had in my closet.

It was just another symbol of how far I had come, even though I still remembered where I once was.

I decided to work on my boxing today, knowing that I had a little too much adrenaline pumping through me to just use weights or even go on the treadmill. Plus, I had run hard the day before, and I didn't want to overdo it.

I wrapped my fists and stretched my shoulders, and then started pounding the bag. I had taken classes so I knew the right way to fight, and not just the way I had learned on the streets when I was a kid.

I tried so hard to remember the best way to do it, rather than the way I had learned at first. I felt like I had punched and pounded those incorrect ways out of my system. Though I knew if I let loose, I'd just fall back into the fight, and those old moves would come back.

I focused on each movement, on each sensation of my fist hitting the bag, and tried to let out all of the anger, the guilt, and the sadness that came with the dreams that just wouldn't go away.

Sweat poured down my body, and by the time I finished my workout, I knew I'd probably be sore later. But it was worth it.

I quickly cleaned up the area, unwrapped my hands, checked for any cuts or abrasions since I was pretty sure I had nicked something and then cursed when I noticed the blood on one of my knuckles.

Yeah, maybe I'd gone a little too hard, but I didn't break anything, so it was worth it.

I quickly cleaned the cut then took a shower, knowing I had to clean it again afterwards, but I wanted to be safe. The last thing I needed was an infection because I couldn't stop having nightmares about my dead best friend.

I let out a sigh, wondering when I had gotten so callous even in my own head. Then I got ready for the day and headed into work.

I walked past Moyer's empty office again and tried to tell myself that it wasn't his office anymore. Someone else worked there now, even if they weren't here today.

Fran gave me a knowing look, and I had a feeling that she knew exactly what I was thinking, so I nodded at her and then went back to my desk.

I hadn't stopped at the coffee shop. Instead, I used the coffee maker in my office to make myself a cup.

I hadn't wanted to risk seeing Harmony again and accidentally having thoughts I shouldn't, or even just thinking about Moyer. Because I'd had enough of that already this morning, and I needed to focus on the here and now. Because focusing on Harmony wasn't going to help anything.

I got through my workday and then rolled my shoulders back, knowing I still had a few more papers to go through, but I would get to that later. Instead, I got in my car and headed to the brewery.

I loved this place, had always loved it. It had been like another home to me, an extension of the one that Jack and Rose had raised us in.

It probably helped that my brothers and I were actually running it now and doing a better job of it than we had in the past. We weren't failing as badly as we had before, and I counted that as a win.

Beckham was behind the bar, and Cameron was working the tables, our waitress not on until later that night. I nodded at them, knowing I looked like I hadn't slept well and was still in my suit from my day job. But it wasn't like I could really go home and change, nor did I want to. I felt better in a crisp suit. I felt more like myself.

"About time you showed up," Cameron said, winking. I knew he was kidding, but I was still slightly on edge from the morning, so I scowled.

"Hey, I have another job. Get off my back."

Cameron's brows rose, and then he shook his head. "I was just messing with you, man. You okay?" Cameron came up to me and studied my face. "You don't have to stay tonight. Aiden's in the back, and between me, Beckham, and Dillon, we've got it. Hell, if we can't handle it after Sandy gets here, I'm sure I can put Violet to work."

Violet was sitting at a table drinking water and snacking on one of the tapas that Aiden had made as she pored over her own work. I knew she was a chemist of some sort, so she probably wasn't actually bringing all of her work with her, but maybe there was paperwork she had to do or something.

"Hey, I have to work on this. And I really just came here to watch you move around in those jeans of yours." She winked, and Cameron rolled his eyes.

"You're talking about me, aren't you?" I said, teasing. "It's okay, we don't have to hide it anymore from Cameron. But I do have to change into my jeans. Even though I know you like me in a suit."

Violet put the back of her hand up to her forehead and leaned back in the booth. "How could you tell him like that, Brendon? I mean, come on, that was just our little secret. And you know I like you better in a suit. With all those nice lines and the way your jacket tucks in just right."

I started laughing as Cameron came up and smacked a hard kiss on Violet's lips before getting up and elbowing me in the gut. I let out an *oof* but still kept laughing.

"I know it's a joke, but let's not do that. Because I'll

have to kick your ass, and I'm really not in the mood for that."

"Hey, I could kick your ass," I said as I lifted my fists to mock fight him.

Cameron's eyes danced before they narrowed on the cut on my knuckle. He frowned. "You okay? What happened?"

I shook my head and flicked out my hand. "Working out this morning. Apparently, I got a little too rough. But don't worry about me. Is Dillon here?"

Cameron didn't blast me on my change of subject, but I knew that he would be watching me. Apparently, now that Cameron was all happy and in a relationship and his life was going well, his new goal was to make sure the rest of us were doing okay. I wasn't sure I really liked that, especially considering that I was the oldest brother and it was *my* job to do so. But I couldn't really stop him either.

"Kid's in the back, finishing up some paperwork for school. And then he's going to be helping Aiden in the kitchen until we need him up front."

"Glad he still wants to do the whole cooking thing. I was afraid that he'd change his mind, and then Aiden would get all growly."

"Aiden is always growly, and Dillon wanting to cook or not won't change that. But Dillon seems like he's having a good time, and Aiden's actually really good at teaching." Cameron just shrugged. "Who would have thought?"

"Probably Jack and Rose," I said softly, and then Cameron met my gaze.

Yeah, our family was fucked-up, but we were getting better.

We were all getting better. It just took time, though sometimes it felt like we didn't have enough of it.

As I talked to Cameron a bit more and then said my goodbyes so I could go up to the office and go over paperwork, I knew that we were getting better.

We were Connollys, and even though we had run away when we shouldn't have before, we weren't going to do that again. We weren't going to give up. We wouldn't be the people we used to be.

And that meant we had to make sure that we stayed together. No matter what. Which meant I had to stop having these dreams that felt like they were taking so much out of me.

And I really had to stop having feelings and thoughts about the one person I shouldn't. Even if that thing seemed more insurmountable than the rest.

CHAPTER FIVE

Death requires so much paperwork. They never tell the living that, do they?

- Harmony to Moyer. 6 months ATE.

HARMONY

SOME DAYS WERE HARDER than others, but the days where I could try to do something good, even when it didn't feel like there was much good in the world, made up for those days.

I sat behind my desk, looking over paperwork as I

entered numbers into a spreadsheet on my computer and emailed people back, going through multiple threads in multiple correspondences.

My job wasn't easy, and it really wasn't undemanding on days like this.

I ran a nonprofit in conjunction with charities, trying to ensure that two local centers and homes for abused women and their families could thrive. I tried to make safe places available. We had multiple spots around the city, and even some across different areas of the state, but there were two main ones that I worked with on an almost daily basis. When I wasn't running the board or trying to coordinate the next event to get more money into the system, or constantly trying to make sure that all of our legal information was up-to-date and our tax things were working out, I was volunteering at the shelters themselves. Or doing every other little part of my job that meant I was dealing with bureaucracy rather than humans.

I knew that despite the horrible events that I had lived through, I was lucky.

I knew that. I knew that things could be so much worse.

I realized that I had been blessed and was lucky that I'd had Moyer. He had never raised a hand to me, never treated me like I was nothing.

We were equals.

He never truly yelled at me. Yes, he'd raised his voice, but then again, so had I. You couldn't go through a whole relationship where you loved every ounce of each other without getting a little annoyed. He never put me down, never made me feel less than.

I knew I was lucky. Fortunate to have had those few years with Moyer.

The women in the shelters hadn't been so lucky.

I was doing everything I could to make sure they had opportunities to stay safe and find ways out of their horrors, as well as ways to separate and try to build new lives.

None of that was made easy when one of my largest contributors decided to back out at the last minute.

Apparently, they did not want to deal with me anymore, and the new tax laws had made the way they would get write-offs a little different. So, they said they were going to save their money and use it in other places. In other words, for things that didn't help women and weren't run by women.

I closed my eyes, pinching the bridge of my nose.

I hated this part of the job. I had money, I gave money. But I had to ask for it daily. I had to do it in ways that didn't come off as begging because that's what people expected. If I had to go down on my knees and beg for money to help others, I would do it in a heartbeat. It just wasn't what others responded to at the moment.

Losing the Jacobs account and the ways they had helped in the past burned.

The original Jacobs, who I'd known for years and who had offered to help had passed away last year. I had known the elder Jacobs through my parents, and the family had come to *my* family's dinner parties over the years.

I had somewhat grown up with their children, the ones who now ran the family business and accounts. By *somewhat*, I meant that while we had been forced to attend the parties, I hadn't gone to school with them. Those children had gone to private schools, while my family had wanted to make sure I got the best education, and that meant going to the school that was closest to me because of their programs.

If the best education in the area had been a private school, I was sure my parents would have sent me there. I just got really lucky.

I kept telling myself I was lucky.

Even if some parts of my life weren't.

But the Jacobs children, who weren't really children anymore since they were a couple of years older than me and into their thirties, did not want to deal with me or my nonprofit. They wanted to send their money elsewhere. And I knew exactly why.

They wanted to help the local boys' club. And the local wine club.

Because that's exactly who needs the money.

I closed my eyes and cursed under my breath.

No, I had to stop thinking like that. Because it wasn't my place to say where anybody spent their money or donated.

I had to draw a line somewhere, and my anger couldn't be directed at whom they were helping. It should be because I knew that the Jacobs family wasn't helping us because of their pettiness.

I remembered Martin Jacobs. The son who was now the oldest of the bunch and head of the family. He had been an annoying nuisance who tried to look up girls' skirts and sneered and slut-shamed girls who rejected him. He had done some despicable things—although never to me.

Though he'd had a few slaps on the wrist, nobody had really cared. Nobody gave a damn because he was privileged. Because he had money. My family cared, my friends cared, but we hadn't been enough to help anyone else.

Now, Martin was using his title and position to pull the funding from my organization.

I would just have to live with it.

That meant I spent the entirety of my day trying to find new donors while organizing a gala and a few other charitable celebrations and events that could bring in money. Sometimes, it was easier to just ask for a check. Other times, I had to go through the song and dance to make things happen. This was the life I had chosen, this was my company. And I was going to make it work. I was going to stop complaining and just get it done.

I really needed coffee.

"I have a few more places for you to look," Eleanor said as she walked in, leaning heavily on her cane.

I looked up and quickly got up from my desk to help her walk into the room, then I sat her down in the chair across from mine and took the papers she held from her.

"You know you're not supposed to put too much weight on that knee," I said, just slightly needling.

"I know, but you needed these, and I want to help as much as I can. If I could go spank that Jacobs man, I would. He deserves being hit with my cane." She winked, and I rolled my eyes.

"You know we do not threaten with violence. There's enough of that out in the world—as is clear, considering what we do."

"I know. But sometimes, I just want to break my oath and hit him with my cane just once."

I shook my head and took the papers back to the other side of the desk.

"Thanks for these," I said softly, looking over the names. Eleanor had been with me since the beginning. She was older than my grandma, yet spry. Well, at least she used to be. She had hurt her knee line dancing of all things, but she was getting back up to snuff.

She had helped me build my organization, brick by brick, donation by donation. She came from money, just as I did, but unlike me, she had been in a marriage where her husband liked to use his fists rather than his words.

She had gotten a divorce at a time when people did not get divorced, especially not in her circles. Her husband had tried to take all of her money, even though he had come from a wealthy family himself, but she refused to let him hurt her anymore.

It had been a big deal back in the day, and I still thought it was. She was so strong, and she had won her case, kept her money, and then donated most of it to help others who couldn't help themselves.

Now, she worked with me most days, even though I told her to go home because she was hurting. Somehow, we were making this place work. It was just a little hard some days, like today, when the rug seemed to be pulled out from under our feet.

The money from the Jacobs family had been

earmarked for the shelter to help with diapers and food and other essentials.

It just angered me to no end that something we had relied upon was now out of our hands because of what I was sure was petty vindictiveness.

"You're getting that frown between your eyebrows again. Stop thinking about that boy if we're not allowed to hit him with my cane. We don't need that. There are plenty of other generous people out there. We'll make do. We always do."

I looked up at Eleanor and wiped away a stray tear that I didn't know had fallen. I hated the fact that I was going to let down people who relied on me.

"I hate this. I really do. I knew things were going too well recently."

"Of course, they were. Because there are generous, amazing people out there. And there will be more. We'll be okay for a while. And that stack of papers I gave you has some amazing people that I know will be able to help. Then, we'll run the next gala and the next charity drive. We'll just keep going like we always do. You're doing good work here, Harmony. You've always been an amazing girl. We'll make do."

"Okay, now you're really going to make me cry," I said, wiping my face. "Okay. I allowed myself to wallow in pity for a little bit and let myself get angry. Now, let's use all of that and push it through to get the job done. Because we will. We are good at what we do."

"Damn straight," Eleanor said with a grin. "However, it is almost lunchtime, and you need to head out."

My brows rose. "What? How can it almost be lunchtime?" I looked at my phone and sighed. "Darn it, I forgot I had plans."

"You have plans with that nice boy, Brendon, right?" Eleanor's eyes filled with a look of glee, and I shook my head.

"Don't start thinking that. He's just a friend. And, yes, we had plans for lunch because we're both trying to get out of our offices more. He's working too hard. I actually offered to have lunch with him today so he wouldn't over-work himself, and now look. I'm the one who's stressed out and should probably cancel."

Eleanor shook her head and then got out of her chair, leaning on her cane again. "Eleanor, sit back down."

"I will sit down once you put things away and head out to lunch. You need this. You need time to just breathe, and Brendon is a very nice boy. I remember."

"You met him once. He's not a boy, and it's not like that. He's just a friend." I let out a sigh. "He was Moyer's friend, Eleanor. It's nice to just have friends. I don't need anything more."

I knew I wasn't lying exactly, but it was getting harder

and harder to say that. Not about Brendon, he *was* just a friend, but about not being alone. Maybe I needed something more. I had gone out on a date, after all. I was taking steps.

But knowing that I was alone was starting to be more evident in my life, turning things a little starker.

"Whatever you say, Harmony. But go to lunch, don't drink too much, and then come back and work. I'll take my break when you get back because I had a late breakfast. We will get this done. But you're so angry and stressed over the Jacobs account that I know you're not going to work as efficiently as you can until you get something to eat and just let it all out."

I knew she was right, so I packed up my stuff, kissed the other woman on the cheek, and headed out. I was running about five minutes late, but I didn't text Brendon, mostly because I was only down the street from the restaurant we were meeting at, and I didn't want to be even later by stopping to text.

I crossed the crosswalk and held in a shiver—as I did every time I did so.

This wasn't where Moyer had been killed, but every time I crossed a street, I remembered. And it hurt. Considering that I worked in downtown Denver, I used a lot of crosswalks like this. Because of that, it didn't feel as bad as it had that first time. Or the first twenty, at least.

Brendon was just walking into the restaurant as I did, and he smiled brightly.

"I was running late, but I got here as quickly as I could. Sorry." He hugged me, one of those Brendon hugs that I sank into.

"I'm running late, too. But, apparently, about the same five minutes you are, so let's call it a wash."

The light in his eyes danced. "Sounds like a plan to me." He searched my face and then frowned. "What's wrong?"

Damn it. The Connolly brothers were far too perceptive sometimes. They were just like my girlfriends, they saw too much, and I couldn't really conceal what I needed to. Not that I wanted to hide everything, but sometimes I didn't want it to be about me. I wanted to learn everyone else's problems so I could help.

"We can talk about it over lunch. However, if there's anything else we could talk about that's a little more fun, I'd love to hear it."

"If you're sure." Brendon squeezed my shoulder and looked at my face again. I just smiled. It felt really good to have him near, to know that I could tell him anything and he'd understand. It was as if I weren't exactly alone, even though I had felt lonely just a few moments ago. Lunch with Brendon would be exactly what I needed. I was glad that I had been pushed out of the office to have it.

Brendon let me go, and we went to the hostess stand before taking our seats. This wasn't a place for reservations at lunch, and I was grateful. I didn't want to do fancy, but this place had good food.

"I'm kind of sad that we aren't going to the brewery for lunch," I said as we sat down.

"The brewery is about five blocks the other way, or we could have. Maybe next time?" Brendon asked as our waiter came by with glasses of water.

"Sounds like a plan to me. And water is fine, thank you," I added to the waiter as he left after handing us our menus.

"So, what should we have?" I asked, looking down at the menu, smiling when I found the last thing on the left side. "Nope, I already picked it out. A chopped Waldorf salad? Amazing."

Brendon just shook his head, laughing. "I swear, you and that salad."

"I can't help it. It's like the most amazing thing in the world."

"I can't believe that trend is coming back, though. You must be happy about that, at least."

"You've got it. What are you going to get?"

"Well, I skipped breakfast other than coffee because I had a long morning, so I'm thinking something greasy and horrible for me. Maybe just a regular bacon cheeseburger? Oh, and onion rings."

I grinned. "That sounds amazing."

He narrowed his gaze at me. "Oh? Well, you can't have an onion ring, I don't share."

I batted my eyelashes. "I might just steal an onion ring because you made it a challenge."

"If you want onion rings, get your own. It's like that meme with the people at the church when the priest or whatever says, 'and do you promise not to steal your husband's fries and to order your own if you want some?' And the woman's like, 'wait was that part of the vows?'"

"I remember that meme," I said, laughing. "And no, that wasn't part of my vows to Moyer. He let me steal the fries."

Brendon just shook his head, his shoulders going back. "Well, I'm not Moyer. You want onion rings, you have to get them yourself."

"Okay..." And so, when the waiter came by, I ordered a salad and a side of onion rings. "There," I said as Brendon kept laughing on the other side of the table. "Now you don't have to share at all, you greedy pig."

"*I'm* the greedy pig? You're the one who's a thief."

"It was just going to be a single onion ring," I said, knowing this was ridiculous. I didn't even really want onion rings, but now it would be a thing, and I was going to eat every single one. "Of course, now I'm going to be fully stuffed and not want to eat dinner later, but it's going to be worth it just to have my own onion rings so you don't pout."

"I do not pout. Connollys do not pout."

"I beg to differ. I've seen Aiden pout a few times when we go back to the kitchen and nothing is perfect enough for him or if we try to steal an onion ring from his plate. Oh my God, is it all of you Connollys? Are you all so stressed about people stealing food off your plates?"

A look of something came over his face, and Brendon swallowed hard. I thought maybe I had said the wrong thing.

"I'm so sorry, what did I do? Are you okay?"

Brendon just smiled, but it didn't reach his eyes. "All of us do have little issues with food, but I think it comes from the whole foster system thing and living on the streets."

I closed my eyes and let out a little curse. "I'm so sorry. I remember that. I know we all talked about it before, I just didn't put two and two together. Considering what I do for a living, that was inconsiderate of me. I'm sorry for making fun of you."

Brendon reached out and gripped my hand, giving it a squeeze that made my stomach clench just a little before he let go. "You have nothing to apologize for. I was always going to let you have an onion ring, Harmony. You're welcome to anything I have. Always."

I didn't know why he said it like that, or why it made me frown, but I was happy when the conversation moved to work, and I could tell him how stressed I was for the day, and he could do the same. We just talked about work and then our families and then our friends. It was a normal lunch. I couldn't help thinking that maybe I had hurt him, and I was sorry for it. I would have to be better about that and not tease him like perhaps I would with someone else. Because Brendon was special, he always had been. And, somehow, I had forgotten that. Or maybe I had gotten too comfortable.

I never wanted to hurt him, but being with him for lunch just reminded me that it was nice to get out of the office and be with someone who understood you. Who cared.

With him, maybe I wasn't so lonely anymore.

Perhaps I just didn't feel like I was always alone.

CHAPTER SIX

BRENDON

I STARED down at my paperwork, wondering if the stack, as well as the files on my computer, had multiplied in the time it took me to blink. I really did love my job, but sometimes it took a little bit too much out of me.

We were having issues on the account that we were trying to get, but I knew we'd figure it out. We usually did. It was just annoying because I had to rely on others to get things done. But that's why I was the boss, I should be used to it by now. Just because I'd rather micro-manage didn't mean I would actually do it. At least not anymore.

I sipped my coffee, wincing at the temperature. I either needed to get a fresh cup or go back to drinking my water because I knew having too much caffeine in my system would just make me grumpier. And I was already a little grumpy.

I didn't know why, things were all right, other than this particular account taking too long. But then again, when things went okay, that usually meant they were about to go to hell soon.

I pinched the bridge of my nose and tried to focus on what was in front of me rather than anything else. I chugged back the rest of the cold coffee and then got up to get myself some water. I might as well be good and not just live on caffeine.

I only had a couple of hours left, and most of my staff was already gone for the day since it was a long weekend, and I had given them time. Of course, I really hadn't taken much for myself, but I would be going home a little early since I wanted to stop by the bar and make sure that everything was okay there.

Not that they actually needed me there these days— only for the paperwork.

I wasn't the best bartender, something that my brothers and Beckham tended to tell me often, much to their amusement. But I enjoyed at least trying. I liked being near my family, something we hadn't done for too long. We still had our issues, but we were getting better. At least, I hoped so.

So I wanted to go down there, lend a hand, or maybe

just sit and have a beer and hang out with my family. At that thought, I smiled and then looked down at my paperwork, knowing I just needed to work a little bit more and then I could relax. At least as much as I *could* when I was at work.

The fact that I kept telling myself that while at a job I used to love told me that maybe I was either working too hard or I had other things going on that were stressing me out. I just didn't know what they were. But I knew at least subconsciously that they would come out of the woodwork soon, and I would have to deal.

By the time I packed up and made it to the bar, it was just before dinnertime, and the slow trickle of the late-afternoon lunch and early dinner crowds were coming in. That made me smile. Because just a few months ago, there hadn't been a trickle at all. There'd been maybe one or two people at this point in the day. But now, the tables were filling up, and I knew we'd have a wait later tonight. Not too bad for a place that we were all afraid would close down.

I'd been so worried that we were going to lose Jack's legacy—our father's legacy.

I didn't know why all of us called them Jack and Rose. If I really thought about it, it was probably because their names were fun to us and it tied in with the bar. There was that sign above the bathroom that would remain no matter what happened to the place. It said *I'll never let you go...unless you need to.*

That just made me smile because Jack and Rose were indeed a happily married couple, and they had been married long before Kate Winslet and Leonardo DiCaprio became the pinnacle Jack and Rose on the big screen.

At least the pinnacle for everyone else. Our Jack and Rose had taken in three foster kids from the street and loved them and made them their own. They would always be the best of the best to us.

So, yes, we did call them Jack and Rose, and sometimes Mom and Dad. It was never a slight to call them by their first names, mostly because that's what they had wanted at first, and then it just stuck. They were Mom and Dad at important times. They had been Mom and Dad when we lost them.

But they were Jack and Rose when we talked about the bar. And that made me feel like maybe we were doing something right. Because the bar was about the two people who had taken us in but took care of what they loved outside of that, as well. At home, they were different. They weren't bar owners. They were parents. And the fact that I talked about them as who they were when I talked about the place that used to be theirs? I knew that was right.

"Hey, you're here," Cameron said from behind the bar as he pulled two drafts. He slid them down the bar top to the two people waiting and then went to enter the order into the computer.

I shrugged off my coat and slid it onto the hook behind the bar before going to the sink and washing my hands.

"Anything I can help with?" I asked, rolling up my sleeves.

"We're not that busy yet, and you know you're better at waiting tables than being behind this bar."

"He's not wrong," Beckham said as he came into the bar area, his arms laden with two racks of glasses.

"I'm not that bad of a bartender. I don't know why you think that."

"It's probably a thing because you get ruffled up like a little peacock," Cameron said, grinning before starting on another draft for another customer.

"I am not a peacock. Why is that the animal you chose? Really? A ruffled-up peacock is the best you can do?"

"I wouldn't start on him," Aiden said as he came into the bar area and picked up a glass so he could get a soda. "I mean, give Cameron and Beckham enough time, and they'll come up with something that pisses you off. You really don't want that. But, don't come back into the kitchen either. You upset the chef, too. Maybe you can take Dillon's job busing and waiting tables. I'll take the kid back and show him the ropes, and you can do what you're good at." Aiden winked, took a sip of his soda, and then went back towards the kitchen. Since his back was to me, he didn't see me flip him off, but everyone else did and laughed.

"Very professional, brother," Cameron said, winking. "Do you do that to all of us when our backs are turned?"

"Just as much as you flip me off. It's sort of a family thing."

"I just love seeing you guys together," Ed said from his spot at the bar after he'd sipped his beer. Ed was a long-time customer who hadn't left when Jack died. He had known Jack and Rose before all of us were even part of the family. And he'd stayed, while others had left.

And that meant that he got free wings every once in a while. But I didn't think that was why Ed kept coming. He came because he liked routine, and he enjoyed the bar. And, hopefully, he liked us.

"Some days are harder than others," I said, shaking my head. "I'm going to the back to look over the books, but if you need me, I'll come and wait tables." I drawled out the last bit, and Cameron and Beckham just laughed. Well, Cameron laughed. Beckham just smiled before going back to his work. The man was always quiet, and I had no idea what really went on beneath that beard of his. So, because nobody wanted me behind the bar—something that I had known would happen as soon as I walked in—I went back to the office and looked over the books.

We had an accountant, but I was the one who got everything ready for them. I probably could have done the accounting on my own, but I'd rather have an actual professional who knew what they were doing for tax purposes.

However, somebody needed to keep up with the daily things and make sure we were on the right track. There were other plans in the works to help the bar stay in the black and increase our revenue—things like specials, ads, and branding.

We had another pool tournament coming up, although us Connollys weren't really joining in. I had a feeling that Aiden and Sienna might want to play because they had been disqualified the first time and wanted to reclaim at least a bit of the dignity they thought they'd lost.

But I didn't think the rest of us were really in the mood to do it. It didn't matter though, because the other bar owners would be joining in again, as would some of the patrons who wanted to show off their skills. That was fine with me since there was a fee to enter, and that meant more beer flowing and food being served every night. The food part was always a little tricky because people wanted bar food, but sometimes they wanted something that wasn't just onion rings or nachos or wings.

That's where Aiden stepped up to the plate. Since we'd been back in Denver, or at least at this place, Aiden had added more things to the menu, constantly changing up some of the appetizers for specials. I knew that had pissed off some of the staff, but in reality, it really wasn't that different every day, and Aiden plainly wrote it out for them. And if my waitresses and waiters couldn't figure out one new menu item each night, then maybe they shouldn't work here.

Dillon had figured it out just fine and was doing great, even though I knew his hours would be changing completely soon because he would be in school. Dillon was going to the University of Colorado at Denver, the same place Cameron's girlfriend, Violet worked. Although, they likely wouldn't ever see each other since Violet worked in the science building, and Dillon would be working on his gen-ed classes.

Maybe even some business classes, though I wasn't exactly sure what he would be taking yet. That reminded me that we needed to figure out his class schedule in the next week or so, so I jotted everything down.

Dillon probably already had it all done on his own, the kid was whip-smart. Sometimes, it was hard for me to remember that even though he had just come into my life and technically wasn't related to me like he was to Cameron and Aiden, the kid was family, and I couldn't actually control him like I wanted to.

Control wasn't the best word for that. No, I just wanted to make sure he had every opportunity available to him. He hadn't had a lot of those growing up, not until Cameron came into his life.

I winced as I unlocked my jaw, unaware that I was so tense. I hated that we'd missed out on so much of Dillon's life due to our lack of communication and our petty disagreements.

It was my fault, just like it was Aiden's and Cameron's, that we'd split up and stopped talking to each other. Things were better now, fucking amazing even, but we still had to work on not being idiots.

I knew we would be better at that, though. Because we had made that mistake once, and we weren't going to do it again. We were different people now. Stronger. And I refused to lose out on time with my brothers and this new friendship we had with the others. I refused.

I pinched the bridge of my nose. I just needed to be okay and live in the moment. I was about twenty minutes into my work when the door opened, and Dillon popped his head in.

"You decent in there?" the kid asked, and I rolled my

eyes just like he often did. Apparently, Dillon was rubbing off on all of us.

The fact that he was eighteen and we still called him *kid* just reminded me that I was getting older. It didn't matter that I was only almost thirty, I was still the oldest of the bunch of us.

And I felt it in my bones. Well, not really, but I knew that day would come. Apparently, almost reaching thirty was the pinnacle where you realized that maybe you were just a little old.

"Decent? I guess so."

Dillon grinned and walked in, a beer in one hand and a swagger to his step.

My brows rose. "Drinking a little early, aren't you? If an undercover cop comes in here and sees you with that beer in your hand outside of the restaurant area, we're shut down."

"That's not true. Plus, my lips have gone nowhere near this. I'm not going to ruin Jack and Rose's place just because it'd be good. Not that I've ever actually had a beer, I've been sweet. Innocent. A saint."

I snorted and then took the beer from him. "Sure. You keep telling yourself that. Because you know what? Cameron, Aiden, and I were perfectly sweet and innocent, as well."

This time, it was Dillon who rolled his eyes.

"Cameron's told me some stuff, so I'm going to go with not so innocent."

I set down the beer and shook my head. "No, we were really good. Well, once we moved under Jack and Rose's roof, we were. I mean, we could have been better, but we weren't bad."

"Ah, that middle of the road. But I swear, I haven't had a sip of that beer. I'm not going to screw things up. I promise."

I leaned back in my chair, nodding. "I believe you. I know that things were a little iffy at first with how you were going to work things out here, but you're doing well. I promise."

"Yeah, good enough to realize that starting school in the spring is kind of stupid, don't you think?"

I frowned and then looked up at him. "What do you mean? You don't want to go to school anymore?"

Dillon stuffed his hands into his jeans' pockets and shrugged. "No, I want to go. I should have gone in the first place. It's more about the whole out-of-state tuition thing. Cameron and I still have a year left to live here. Because even though he's not technically my dad, he was my guardian for long enough that they're taking his California residence into consideration. And we haven't lived here for a full year yet. That means we have a semester of out-of-state tuition before we can apply for in-state. And that's not cheap."

I sighed, closing my eyes. "It's not. It's a little ridiculous. But the states want their students to go and stay in school in their own states. Therefore, they give them incentives. I know it's ridiculous, but you're not going to the main campus, just UCD. Not that there's anything *just* about it. The school's amazing. Violet wouldn't be working there if it didn't have a great program."

"I'm not exactly in her program," Dillon countered.

"No, you're not going into science, but you are taking gen-ed classes. And we can look into you going to one of the community colleges instead. There's still time."

Dillon shrugged. "Maybe that would have been smart. But I kind of wanted to get into a university because I screwed up so badly in the first place. You know?"

I understood. I got up from behind the desk and moved forward to put my hand on the kid's shoulder. He didn't flinch, didn't back away. I took that as a good sign. Because even at Dillon's age, any of the three of us would have flinched. We had been through shit, and Dillon had a little bit as well, but Cameron had shielded him from the worst of it. And for that, I would be forever grateful to my brother.

"You screwed up, but you're fixing it. If you want to go

to the University of Colorado at Denver, then we'll pay for it. You don't need to worry about that. You had good grades and are currently showing a fantastic work ethic. You do need to worry about keeping your job and keeping up your grades, though. Because if you fail, then you're fucked. Because we're not going to bail you out. So, you need to work your ass off. If you do, you'll be fine. Yeah, a semester of out-of-state tuition won't be the nicest thing in the world, but I've got money, and so does Cameron. And I bet Aiden does too, though he hoards it all like a little dragon."

"I thought you were the dragon that hoards things?" Dillon said, grinning.

"That may be true. Connolly dragons, I kind of like the sound of that, it has a nice ring to it."

"Maybe we can get like a little mascot or something for the bar."

I snorted. "You know, that doesn't sound like too bad of an idea. Okay, why don't I take this beer that you just painstakingly brought to me, and we can go down to the bar so I can help out? I probably shouldn't be drinking on the job anyway."

"Cameron's the one who sent it up. Said that you're supposed to take the day off because you already worked a full shift at your other job."

I sighed and took a sip, holding in a moan at the taste.

It was one of Cameron's new brews, and I was in love. "Maybe taking a day off would be fine."

"And a single beer isn't going to screw you up in case we get busy."

"Speaking of busy, you'd better get back down there before Cameron or Aiden finds a reason to start yelling."

"It would be Aiden that would yell first. Right?"

I sighed. "Yep. He's the one with the temper, even though most people think it's Cameron."

"It's the twin thing, isn't it?"

I nodded and then followed Dillon back into the bar area. Aiden and Cameron were twins, though they had spent some of their youth split apart in different foster homes. And though I was the oldest brother, I was the one not related by blood to any of them. But we were all brothers. No matter what.

I set my beer back on the work table in the corner, one that we only filled with customers when the place was packed. I looked out at everyone milling around and figured we might reach capacity tonight. I smiled. It sounded like a good plan to me.

I let the stress of both jobs leave my mind, then the sadness that had been filling me regarding my friend who was no longer here, and the woman whom he'd left behind, as well. I didn't think about Moyer that often, but now that I really thought about it, I was doing it more often of late. I just wanted to relax and not think about anything.

"Hey, Brendon," Beckham called out. "There's someone here looking for you."

I sat up a little straighter, thinking for a moment that it might be Harmony. I didn't know why that was the first thought that came to mind, but it would have been nice to see her. Although I didn't know if she was coming in tonight at all. I missed her, and it had only been a day since I'd seen her. That probably meant I needed to put some distance between us, but I wasn't always a smart man.

I moved up to the front of the bar, looking around for Harmony and then freezing when I saw exactly who was at the other end of the bar.

"What are you doing here?" I said the words, my voice wooden, emotionless.

Because I knew who it was. I just hadn't seen him in years.

Hadn't even known if he was still alive. But do they tell you when your estranged dad dies? Do they tell you any of that?

Do they somehow find your adult children after you die even if you were a lowlife piece of shit?

I didn't think they did. But then again, I didn't really trust the system anymore. I hadn't when I was younger, forced to do things I'd rather not talk or even think about. The system had failed me more times than I could count, and the only time they'd ever done anything good for me was when they brought me to Jack and Rose.

Now I looked at the man who had sold me for drugs and wondered what the fuck was wrong with my life that this could happen.

I'd known I was too happy.

I had known that things were going okay, and I was smiling more than I had been before. I knew the nightmares were there, but I hadn't picked up my go-bag in a long time. Of course, things were going too well.

And, of course, things were here to fuck it all up.

"I just want to talk, son."

I held up my hand, rage filling me even through the void of coldness. "Don't call me that. I'm not your son."

"Okay." Sam nodded quickly. His eyes darted around, and I knew others were watching, even though I wasn't raising my voice. I was trying not to make a scene, but it wasn't easy when this asshole was in front of me.

"You need to go." I forced out the words, trying not to scream.

I was aware that Cameron, Aiden, Beckham, and even Dillon were around, watching, waiting. And I didn't want to talk to anyone. Didn't want to do anything.

So, I took a right, went to get my jacket from behind the bar, and left without another word.

Sam wasn't supposed to be there. But if he was, I couldn't be, not under the same roof.

It was either leave or try to rip out the man's heart. And I wasn't even sure he had one.

Bile filled my throat, and I was aware that Cameron was running after me, shouting my name.

But I didn't care. I just needed to go home, needed to get away from it all. I needed to take a shower. Do something. As long as I was clean, everything would be fine. He wouldn't touch me again.

That man was from my past. It was all in my past.

And I wasn't going to let it touch my present.

I wasn't going to let it touch *me*.

Not anymore.

CHAPTER SEVEN

I miss boring dates. I miss cuddling on the couch. I just miss you.

- Harmony to Moyer. 2 months ATE.

HARMONY

TONIGHT WAS ROUND TWO. Or perhaps it was just part two of round one. Who knows? I wasn't really good at boxing metaphors, and I figured I should probably stop and start something new. After all, this was my first date with another man. My second first date since deciding that I needed to get out of the house and learn to live amongst others again.

This man was named Tim. He was sweet. He had a slightly weak jaw, but not everybody could have a perfect jaw. He had kind eyes, though they did wander while we were talking sometimes as if he got distracted or wasn't really paying attention to me. Maybe I was just reading too much into it, and he could multitask. After all, he was a computer analyst, he probably did that every day.

Multiple times a day.

So, him not looking at me while we were talking was probably just fine.

A point in his favor, however, was that when I ordered my rosemary chicken with a side of creamy mashed potatoes and buttery broccoli, he didn't say a word. Hadn't commented about the butter, or the starches, or about the martini I had ordered instead of wine.

He hadn't said anything at all.

In fact, I wasn't really sure if he even noticed I had eaten.

But it was just a first date, and I had to stop being so overly critical.

"So, you've lived in Denver your whole life then?" I asked, playing with my potatoes. I hadn't eaten much, and I was a little too nervous to eat more than I already had. That just meant I'd have leftovers to devour later. I liked food, and I hated wasting it, but I also couldn't eat when I felt like I was doing something wrong.

Why was this date so boring? Did I just hang too much on it? Or maybe I just remembered the good ones I used to have and was trying to compare them. I couldn't. This was a different time. Dating had changed so much, even in the last few years, and I wasn't very good at it, apparently. This time, I was on a date set up by another friend at work, one who said Tim would be perfect for me. Now, I was questioning my choices in all manner of things. Like why was she even working for me if she thought Tim would be perfect for me?

I needed to stop thinking like that. Everything was fine. I was just stressing out for no reason.

Tim cleared his throat. Again. How much phlegm could the man actually have? It seemed it was all he kept doing. It was like there was something lodged in there, and he couldn't quite cough it out.

Every time he spoke, even in between sentences or in the middle of a sentence, he cleared his throat. I didn't really understand it, but I had to stop being so picky.

So judgmental.

But when he did it again, I just smiled, holding back my wince.

I was doing this whole dating thing wrong. Why was I doing this again?

"Yes, I've lived in Arvada my whole life. My parents actually live next door. It was just luck that the Andersons moved out and I could purchase the house next to theirs. It's nice being so close. I mean, I lived in their home for most of my life, so having a place of my own is a little easier. Especially if I ever have a date." He winked and then cleared his throat. Again. I had to suppress the wince.

A wink, just like my first date, *and* clearing his throat. Apparently, every man had a tic that I was going to find and get annoyed with. This was all on me, not him. He was nice.

And then I frowned, going back over his words. "You live next door to your parents? That's actually quite nice. I wished I lived closer to mine, even though we live in the same city. But even with the suburbs being so close together, sometimes it can take up to an hour to get there with traffic."

Tim smiled. His eyes were quite nice, very kind. I had to remember that.

"Oh, yeah, I love living next to them. I mean, it was easier to get food and my laundry done when I was actually living with them, but the past couple of years living outside the home, it's been kind of nice having my independence. But Mom does come over to help me with the laundry and stuff. And it's just easier for her to fill my fridge if she actually has the key. You know? I mean, I'm really busy, and she really loves doing it. My mom's an amazing woman."

Oh. Great. Apparently, he'd lived with his mother until he was twenty-eight. In this economy, that actually wasn't that bad. I was very lucky in my station, in my family. I knew that. Other than losing my best friend and my husband, my life had actually been quite nice.

Yes, those two shadows broke me time and again, but I was okay. And, yes, I kept telling myself that, but it was a coping mechanism, and it had worked just fine for the last two years.

However, it didn't sound as if Tim had stayed with his parents for financial reasons. Not with his job. I knew through my co-worker that Tim had been working in his high-income job for longer than he had lived outside of his parents' home.

I couldn't help but judge him just a bit, and I hated myself for it.

Just because he'd lived with his parents up until recently didn't mean that he had leeched off of them. It didn't mean that he was one of the clichéd kids living in his parents' basement.

"I'm glad that you have your own home now. It must be nice."

"Oh, it is, but sometimes I wish I could just move back

there. You know? It's just so hard to do everything on my own. But I'm lucky that my mom likes to take care of most things for me. You know what I mean?"

No, I really didn't know what he meant. And I was a little confused. "I suppose. But you have your own place, you have a great job. And now you get to come out and hang out in the city."

"Oh, yeah, I don't really go out to dinner much. At least, not with women. You know? I am not really good at the whole dating thing."

Neither was I. But I didn't say that. It was pretty evident.

"Don't worry, I'm getting pretty okay at it."

He leaned forward and put his hand on mine. I resisted the urge to pull back. Just because I didn't really understand his choices and he kind of annoyed me and there was literally no chemistry between us, didn't mean I had to be rude.

"I'm glad you're here tonight. It's nice going out with a woman as beautiful as you are."

"Oh, thanks." What was I supposed to say to that? I felt just as awkward as he seemed, but hopefully, I didn't put out the creepy vibes like he was.

"Anyway, as I was saying, my parents do live next door, but they won't be at my house tonight. So, we'll be all alone. Just the two of us, if you know what I mean." He grinned and leaned forward.

Suddenly, the four or so bites of my meal I'd taken settled in my stomach like a rock. I had no desire to sleep with this man, no desire to see him again actually, especially after this moment.

Were men always so forward like this? Or maybe he wasn't being forward at all, and I was just being ridiculous. I could see that, being ridiculous. I wasn't very good at this dating thing. Maybe I just saw all the bad things at once.

"How's your meal?" I said, deliberately changing the subject.

His kind eyes weren't very nice anymore, the look in them had hardened just a bit. He squeezed my hand, and I quickly moved it away, not wanting his touch anymore.

"My meal is just fine. Did I say something wrong?" And then he looked at me, his eyes going kind, soft, and oh so sickly sweet again. He snapped his fingers. "Oh, right, I forgot. You were married, right? Didn't he die or something? I'm trying to remember what Candace told me. Yeah, he died, right? Oh, shit. Is this your first date since that? Because I don't know if I'm going to be able to live up to that. You know? That's a lot."

I just blinked at him, wondering why Candace would think that this was okay. Clarisse had thought that my other date, Jason, was fine. She had been wrong. Candace believed that Tim would be fine, and she was *definitely* wrong.

My hand shook, and my palms turned clammy.

Tim just kept saying *dead.* Dead and husband, together, over and over again. Or maybe it was only on a loop in my mind.

I knew my husband was dead. I knew he was gone. I lived with it every day of my life. I didn't need a stranger saying it over and over to me, worried that he was going to hurt my feelings. Because he'd already done that. He'd already done way more than that. It didn't make any sense to me. Why was I on a date with this man?

And why would he just snap his fingers and suddenly remember that Moyer was gone? He hadn't even known Moyer.

It felt like I was tarnishing my husband's memory just by being next to Tim.

And so, I wiped my mouth, gave a pleasant smile, and stood up.

"What? Did I say something wrong? I mean, he is dead, right? You're not like cheating on him, are you? Because I'm not into that. But you're free, right?"

I just shook my head, took my purse, and laid out a couple of bills on the table. It looked like I was splitting the bill again. "You're right, Tim, you're really not very good at dating. Yes, my husband is gone, but he's of no concern to you. I will not be going home with you. And you really need to look at your life and wonder why you're relying on your parents so much even though you think you're independent. No, don't open your mouth, don't speak. Because you're lucky I didn't splash the rest of my martini in your face. I would really hate to ruin and waste this drink. And you know what? I was really looking forward to finishing my meal at home when I didn't have to deal with you, but now, I'll just look at it and think about the way you tried to make me feel. The insecurities that came through your mouth as you thought that maybe I would want to be with you were clear. But that's not the case, Tim. It was never the case. And maybe you should learn something about sensitivity, because you're just an ass."

The woman next to me clapped just a little, and so did her friend at the table. I gave them a regal nod, picked up my coat, and sauntered out of the restaurant.

I was shaking, and bile filled my mouth again, but it wasn't because I was scared. It wasn't because I was afraid that Tim would come after me. After all, I'd left him looking like a guppie, his mouth open as if wondering why I would say such cruel things to him.

Maybe he would talk to Candace, and Candace would talk to me, but I didn't care.

Because I wasn't doing this again. I wasn't going on a date with dear old Tim.

Because he was an insensitive jerk, and I had learned long ago to stand up for myself. I wasn't rude, I was just honest. He could go fuck himself.

I'd only had two sips of my martini, so I was just fine to drive home.

I grumbled and waited for the valet to bring my car around.

I was just so angry, so dejected.

Why wasn't I any good at this? I should have been better. Right?

I mean, it was always going to be hard. The idea of me trying to move on after losing my husband was always going to be painful. But why did it have to feel like a joke at the same time?

I didn't feel a single connection to either of the men that I had sat across from at dinner.

I didn't feel any pull, no tug. I didn't feel that clutch in my belly that told me that it might be something. That maybe it wouldn't be serious, but perhaps I could just be happy for the moment.

But I hadn't felt that at all. Maybe most of it was because I was still slightly numb after losing Moyer. I figured I'd always be a bit numb to the world because I had lost him. After all, he had taken part of my heart with him, leaving behind a frozen, pale shadow of who I had been.

And that was fine. We were supposed to scar after the loss of a loved one. We should mark and alter the ones we love wholeheartedly.

I wouldn't be who I was now without Moyer. I wouldn't be the person I was today without the loss of him. I was a different woman with each breath that I took because of the pain that I went through, and because of the love that I felt for him—because he had loved me with every ounce of himself, as well.

And it was okay that I was still trying to find a new version of myself. That I was trying to find happiness again. Maybe not pure bliss, because I wasn't sure that would ever happen again. But I missed companionship, I missed having someone on the other side of the table that could make me smile and make me feel wanted.

I missed that.

And shoring up the courage after two years to even say yes to a date was something that had made me sob in my bathtub.

I had said yes to my first date, then had thrown up, and then had turned on the shower to hot and sank into my tub.

I had let it fill up, and just let myself sit there as the

water beat down on me. After, I sank down into the hot, soothing liquid.

I had tried so hard for so long to act like I was okay. I wasn't. My friends had tried to make sure I understood they saw that. They had done their best to make me understand what I had lost and what I had become.

Going out on a date had seemed so strange, so heart-breaking.

But Violet, Sienna, and even Meadow and Allison had been there for me.

Allison was gone now, and Meadow hadn't known me when I was with Moyer, but when Allison was alive, she had been supportive. And Meadow knew the new me, and she was supportive, as well.

Everybody tried so hard to make sure that I was okay, and I just kept failing at it.

Why did people who wanted me to be happy put me on dates with such terrible men? Were they terrible because they weren't Moyer? I shook my head as I pulled into my driveway. No, that wasn't the case. Because there were good men out there. The Connollys were some of them. The way Cameron cared for Violet told me that there were good men out there—good, caring, wonderful men who didn't stand by when others were in pain.

Brendon and Aiden were that, as well.

Brendon was even there for me now, and he was a person that I could sit across the table from and feel wanted, even if it was just in friendship. He never made me feel like I was less than, like things were awkward because he wasn't Moyer. He was Brendon, he was someone different, and I would be forever grateful that he was back in my life as my friend.

I toed off my shoes as I walked into my house, then took off my earrings and poured myself a glass of wine.

It wasn't even eight at night, far too early to be home from a date, but I was hungry, and the experience had been horrendous. I looked down at my phone and frowned.

I hadn't spoken to Brendon in a couple of days. Maybe I just needed a voice that told me that everything would be okay. Maybe that was selfish, but after a date like the one I'd just had, I needed that.

I would have called one of my girlfriends, but Violet was on a date with Cameron, and I knew Sienna was out with some of her co-workers, celebrating the promotion of one of her work friends.

I didn't know Meadow well enough to call her and talk about nothing in particular, but Brendon was my friend. I was allowed to call him. Right?

Before I thought too hard about it, I pulled out my phone, brought up his contact, and called.

He answered on the second ring, and I sighed in

relief. Brendon would make everything better. I would lean on him, and hopefully, he would lean on me one day.

If the man ever leaned at all.

"Harmony? Is everything okay?" His voice was a bit low as if he had been sleeping or just quiet for too long.

"I'm fine, am I interrupting? I know it's not too late, but you sound as if you were sleeping?"

I could hear him rustling around as if he were sitting up, and I winced. "I wasn't sleeping, just hanging out on the couch doing nothing. Had a long day. You okay, Harmony?"

"I'm fine, I promise. I just went on a really bad date and wanted to talk to a friend. But now I realize that I might be annoying you." I hated how whiny I sounded. I should probably just heat up some leftovers, take a bath, and then go to bed. That would be best for everyone involved. But I had just wanted to hear a friendly voice. Now, I regretted that.

"A bad date? Did he hurt you?" The urgency and anger in Brendon's tone surprised me even though it shouldn't have. Brendon was very protective of his friends, and I tried not to make him think I needed to be protected all the time.

"He didn't hurt me. He was just a butthead. Actually, I think I called him an ass to his face, if that helps.

Brendon barked out a laugh, but I could tell there was

something strained about it. "That's good to hear," he said softly. "Because I'll go kick his ass for you if you want. I can still do that."

"You keep offering to kick asses for me. I don't really know what that means." There was silence, and I wondered what I had said that caused it.

"It just means that I'm here for you, Harmony. I'm sorry the guy was an ass. Did you at least get a good meal out of it?"

This time, I laughed. "Not even close. Couldn't even enjoy my food. And because I was so angry, I didn't even want to look at the food that I had with him. I left it on the table. Meaning I'm about to heat up something and pretend it's the delicious meal I wanted."

"See, now I'm going to have to kick his ass because you don't stand in your way when it comes to food."

"Oh, shut up," I said, laughing again.

"Hey, we don't share food. I know the rules. That's what I like about you, there are boundaries. And we both love food."

"Thanks for making me laugh. Today sucked, but I'm smiling now, so I guess it was good that I called you."

"You're always welcome to call me, Harmony. Always."

There was silence, and I wondered what he was thinking, but it was so hard to tell with him sometimes.

"Is everything okay with you? We've been talking about me for so long that I never really get to ask you how you're feeling."

Silence again.

"Brendon?"

"I'm fine. Just a hard day. I'm sure you're going to hear about it from the others eventually."

I stiffened. "What happened?"

"Nothing I really want to talk about right now, Harmony. Okay?"

"Okay," I said, a little hurt though I didn't know why. "But I'm here if you need me. Our conversations never have to be one-sided, Brendon. You're always there for me, so I hope you know I'm always here for you."

"I know." He mumbled something else, but I didn't hear it.

"What?"

"Nothing. I'm fine, Harmony. You should go eat and relax after your night."

There was something off about him, and I couldn't figure out what it was. But he didn't want to tell me, so I wasn't going to bother him about it.

Maybe he would tell me eventually. And perhaps I'd just get it out of him. Because that's what friends were for, to be there for each other even when you didn't want to talk about things. Because sometimes those things just needed to be aired.

"I'll talk to you tomorrow, okay, Brendon? Because if the others are already going to talk to me about it, I would rather hear about it from you. I know I'm pushing, and I'll stop if you tell me to. I promise."

He sighed. "My birth dad showed up. The guys are probably going to talk to you about it later because that's what we always do, we talk. But I'm fine. Just tired."

"Oh, Brendon." I didn't know much about his birth father, only that Brendon had been pulled into the system and then subsequently placed in Jack and Rose's house around the same time that Aiden and Cameron came to live with them.

I knew that whatever happened had to be bad, something that gave him nightmares, but I never pushed. Because it wasn't my place, even though I hated the fact that he was hurting.

As someone who disliked when all of my business was constantly being aired, and everybody needed to ask me if I was okay or how they could maybe try and fix it even though they couldn't...I understood.

So, I wasn't going to push.

"Just know that I'm here for you," I said quickly. "And I'm not going to ask you anything else. Because if you don't want to talk about it, I'm not going to make you.

Believe me, I won't make you talk about anything you don't want to."

Brendon let out a breath. "I know. I'll talk to you soon, okay? I'm sorry your date sucked. I'm glad you called. I'm always glad when you call, Harmony."

There was that weird clutch.

"Good night, Brendon."

"Good night, Harmony."

He disconnected the call, and I looked down at my phone, wondering if I had messed up.

I never wanted him to feel like I was a burden, and I always wanted to help. But sometimes he just needed space. So, I would give him that, if that's what he needed. And then I would be in his face to make sure he was okay, just like he did for me.

Because he was my friend, and he deserved everything I had.

Even if I didn't know what I had left to give.

CHAPTER EIGHT

BRENDON

I'D SLEPT FOR SHIT, and the nightmares had been the worst they'd ever been. It didn't matter that it was a weekend and I'd tried to sleep in. My body didn't let me. I wasn't sure I'd ever be able to get a full night's sleep again.

Between normal stress dreams of work and the bar and even my brothers, I'd also had nightmares about Sam and then Moyer. At one point, Sam had been the one behind me, holding me back instead of that stupid piece of gum, and I'd had to watch Moyer die again, only while standing next to Sam.

I'd woken up trying to scream without being able to let out a single sound. And because of that, I knew I needed to call my therapist and set up an appointment. It had been a year since I'd gone, but maybe it was time to go again.

It hadn't helped that Harmony had been in some of the dreams, just standing there, right out of reach so I couldn't even talk to her or pull her out of the way so she didn't have to watch what happened to me in the past or Moyer on that street.

I hadn't been able to help her.

I never could.

But they were only dreams, and I'd be fine. I just needed to work this anger and anxiety out of my system. And to do that, I would work out. Then I'd scream into the void or something if I couldn't figure out what to do next.

But first, today I was just going to try and relax, or at least pound out my frustrations. Thankfully, one of my investments just happened to have a way to do that.

"You know, I've never really been good at the whole wall-climbing thing," Cameron said from my side.

I looked over at my brother and frowned. "You have more muscles than any of us." Much to my dismay, but I didn't mention that. "I figured you liked this. You used to do it all the time."

Cameron shook his head, looking up. "No, *you* liked

doing this. And Violet liked doing it too until she hurt her wrist a few years ago."

A look of something washed over his face for just a moment before he blinked it away, and I knew that Cameron was feeling guilty. None of us had really been around when Violet hurt her wrist while out on the trails working and collecting samples for her job. It wasn't a break, but it was just enough strain that she didn't rock climb like she used to. I hadn't even known it was an issue until she mentioned it in passing and the girls had just nodded, having known all along.

We guys hadn't known a thing because we'd all broken apart before. But we were all a unit once more, so the things that we had missed would come back. At least I hoped.

"You should have told me when I invited you to come," I said quickly.

"You called us, we're here," Aiden said, his voice low.

I looked over at my other brother and frowned.

I didn't really know what that meant, but maybe it was because I wasn't looking far or deep enough. After all, they all knew that Sam was back and that I was trying not to think about it. That's what we did, we tried not to think.

It always ended up falling apart in the end, but right now, I just wanted to climb.

"Well, thanks," I said, clearing my throat.

"You ready to do this then?" I asked, looking at my brothers and then up at the rock-climbing wall again. Dillon hadn't wanted to come, mostly because he'd said that the three of us needed our time together. I figured it was because the kid didn't know how to climb the wall, but that would change soon. I didn't mind giving the guy some space. So, Dillon could work with Beckham to open the bar for us so we didn't all have to be there today. Oh, all of us would go in later, but for now, three of the Connollys would let some tension out.

Though since Cameron's shoulders weren't as tense as they probably should be considering that he wasn't a huge fan of rock climbing, I figured that he'd gotten his tension out in other ways.

Aiden and I would just have to climb the damn wall.

"Okay, let's go," I said as we all walked over to the wall and started getting into our harnesses.

There were spotters for us, and we were all geared up. We weren't going to be stupid and try to showboat. I might know what I was doing, and would anchor-free climb at some points, but I wasn't going to risk my life just to act as if I were some fancy shit or something.

We each started off with our own paths, cursing at each other and laughing as one went up one way, the other his way. I was in the middle, laughing as Aiden and

Cameron grunted at each other, each using their hand-holds and footholds so they didn't fall.

I was doing the same, sweat pebbling on my brow as I lifted myself up to the next handhold. I gripped tightly, checking to make sure to hold my weight, and then waited there for a second, trying to catch my breath.

I was in shape, but it had been long enough since I'd done this that I felt like a wet noodle. We would all likely be sore for the rest of the day—and probably for the rest of the week—but it would be a good sore. 'Cause I was still so damned angry.

There was nothing I could do about it, so maybe if I just kept quiet, kept putting my all into the climb, I wouldn't be so angry anymore.

But it pissed me off that Sam thought he could just show up out of nowhere, that he could reset my equilibrium.

I hadn't seen the man since I'd been pulled from his arms when I was a kid.

So even though we had all aged, and Sam looked far older than his years and appeared clean now, I recognized him right away.

Even without the glossy sheen of drugs in his eyes, I recognized him.

Because they were my eyes, just set in a sunken face

of a body that might not have drugs in its system anymore, but that had been weathered by time and bad decisions.

I frowned and reached up for the next handhold, only to slip on my own sweat. I caught myself and cursed as Aiden looked over at me, his brows raised.

"You okay, brother?"

I sighed. "I'm fine. Just missed the handhold. I'll get it next time. Damn it."

Aiden gave me a tight nod, and I looked over my shoulder at Cameron, who was still a couple of feet below me but looking up his own path. I was on the hardest level, but that was because I had the most experience. Cameron was on the easiest, mostly because it had been a while since he'd done this, and now that I knew that Cameron wasn't a big fan, I wondered if maybe we should have gone on the easier wall. But it was too late for that.

One at a time, I wiped my hands on my shirt, blew on them, and then reached up, gripping tightly so I could balance myself again.

I kept cycling through my thoughts, my dreams. There was Sam, then Moyer, then Harmony, and then work, the bar, Jack, and then it was back to Sam, and all I could do was try to push it out of my system, attempt to focus. But it just wasn't going to work.

I was angry enough, ragged enough, that I knew that

no matter what I did, I wasn't going to get over what had happened anytime soon. I would have to face it, and I really fucking hated that idea.

So, I tried my best to push all of those thoughts out of my system so I wouldn't hurt myself, or worse, end up hurting my brothers somehow, and made my way up the wall, one painstaking movement at a time. When I rang the bell, sweat poured down my body, and my muscles ached. I knew I'd hurt later, knew that I had pushed myself too far, but I was in the safety harness.

I slowly lowered myself down as Aiden and Cameron finished their climbs. Aiden made it first, then Cameron, and soon, the three of us were all level with one another, shaking our heads as we looked at each other.

"What the hell were we thinking?" Cameron asked, getting out of his harness with someone's help. "I mean, we did it, and it was kind of great, but what were we thinking?"

Aiden barked out a laugh. "That we're stupid? I don't know. It was Brendon's idea, so I'm just going to blame him." He rolled his shoulder, wincing as he pressed his palm to the joint. "Because this hurts."

"Yeah, maybe we should just start with a beer and less bone-breaking activities to make us feel better," Cameron said, looking directly at me.

I knew they were both waiting for me to blow up or

figure out exactly what was going on, but I didn't know. I was just so angry. And, apparently, there was nothing I could do to get it out of my system. Pushing my body to its limits while rock climbing hadn't helped. Working out before hadn't helped. It seemed nothing would help.

We had all finished taking off our harnesses when I looked over at the second rock wall where a group of what looked like teenagers were laughing and pointing up.

I let out a curse and then ran over, my brothers right behind me.

"What the fuck do you think you're doing?" I shouted as the kid slowly came down the rock wall. He wasn't wearing a harness, wasn't even wearing a helmet. Didn't have on *any* safety gear, and somehow, nobody had fucking noticed.

The kid landed on the ground, and I stormed right to him. I didn't touch him, I wasn't angry enough to actually assault some kid, but I was pissed. He looked to be about Dillon's age, and he could have died.

"Hey, man, we were just messing around. I mean, what the fuck? You're not my dad. Nobody was hurt. Get off, man."

"You think you're funny? You think you can just go and break the rules because you're above everybody? You could've gotten hurt. You could've fallen and cracked your head open, and then your friends wouldn't have been laughing, they'd be screaming about your brains splattered on the floor. Is that what you want? You want to be the big man and end up dead on the floor because you're a dumbass?"

"Brendon," Cameron said, pulling me back. But I didn't budge. I was just so fucking pissed. And, apparently, this kid was getting the worst of it.

"Shut up, asshole. Whatever. No one was hurt."

"Really? You think that's the case? How about you go look over at the younger kids behind you? They were watching you. Now, they're going to go up and think it's okay to climb without a harness or gear. What the fuck were you thinking?"

"I'm not a kid. I'm twenty. I can do what the fuck I want."

"No, you can't. And, in case you didn't know, I actually own this building. So why don't you get the fuck out?"

I didn't show my hand with regards to how much money I had made over my life often. I didn't grandstand or tell others what businesses or buildings I owned. My brothers knew that I owned this place, I just didn't manage it. I was the money man, the one who made the big decisions, though in the end, not all of them.

As the rest of the staff came up, even the manager who had been back in the office, I let them handle it and stomped off, my body shaking.

The kid had wide eyes at my proclamation, but the fact that he was twenty years old, meant he really wasn't a kid. He was a damned man, making stupid decisions.

As I looked down at my callused hands and the fact that I was still shaking, I realized I had made some poor decisions, as well.

"I need a fucking shower," I whispered. Aiden squeezed my shoulder. "Yeah, let's do that. And then let's get to the bar or something because I think you need to talk. Or maybe drink. Or maybe hit something that's not a snot-nosed kid."

"The staff's going to handle it, and they're probably not going to like the fact that you yelled like you did. But you're the owner, I don't think they can really yell at you back."

We stalked to the lockers, and I shook my head. "I deserve it. I shouldn't have blown up like that."

"Well, you're going through a lot right now, and considering you're obviously not dealing with it well, it was bound to happen," Aiden said as he pulled off his shirt. "You know what I mean?"

"Yeah. If you're the one who's trying to talk me down and act reasonable, I guess I really fucked up."

Aiden flipped me off, and I just laughed, even though it wasn't real. I'd let my emotions get the best of me and had taken it out on some kid who, yes, had deserved the tongue-lashing, but not from me. I just hoped that those who saw the kid climb the wall without gear and nobody watching him wouldn't try to do the same.

I'd seen a couple of falls in my day, and I didn't want to see or hear about one again.

I showered, thankful that when the manager and everyone had wanted to remodel, we had installed private stalls. I just let the water run down my body and scrubbed myself until I was bright red, practically bleeding. But I had to get clean. The cleaner I was, the better I could handle whatever was coming.

Yes, I knew my obsessive behavior was an issue. I had seen a therapist about it, but there was no changing it. No getting over it anytime soon.

By the time we made it to the Connolly Brewery, Jack's place, I went straight up to the office, not really wanting to talk to anyone.

Dillon had given us a bunch of looks as he took orders at another table, but he didn't say anything. It was nice to see that at least some of today's youth weren't assholes. And...I was officially an old man. I wasn't even thirty yet, and I had hit old-man stage.

I knew Cameron and Aiden were following me to the office, but then Aiden took a left to the kitchen, probably to make sure that his precious food was taken care of.

Cameron didn't come up right away as I sat down in the desk chair. I was grateful.

I was embarrassed, angry, and I knew I should probably just go home, but I also knew that no one would let me. They didn't want me to be alone, and they wanted to drag my thoughts and feelings out.

I could remember the days when we were younger and hadn't actually spoken about what we were feeling. And then Jack and Rose had forced us to do it daily until I'd wanted to throw up. But I had finally just told them exactly what I was feeling and what was pissing me off.

It'd become routine, but it was something that we'd all gotten out of the habit of after Cameron moved away. But now he was back, and we were trying to be better about it. It was very unlike most guys, but we were Connollys, we weren't like most men.

Or at least what society told us males needed to be.

I pinched the bridge of my nose.

And now I was thinking about society and toxic masculinity rather than actually thinking about what the fuck was wrong with me. I'd reached peak denial, and I was just tired.

"Okay, I have a beer for you, and one for me. It's lunchtime. It's the weekend. It's really okay. Now, though, why don't you tell me what's going on?"

"Don't forget about me," Aiden said, a beer in his own

hand. "I can have one, and then I'm going to eat and then work. But I figured this is a beer conversation."

My brothers took seats in front of me, and I just groaned.

"I'm surprised Dillon isn't here."

"He can be, if you want. He actually asked, but I figured you'd want him out there working, give the three of us some time alone. Kid doesn't really feel like he's a Connolly sometimes, but that's not your problem."

"I think that's part of why my brain hurts."

"I'm going to bet the biggest part of it is Sam," Aiden said, dropping my birth father's name out there like it was nothing.

"Aiden," Cameron warned.

"No, we were good for a whole day. We let him run off after Sam showed up out of nowhere. We let him climb a wall and force us to do it, too."

"I didn't force you," I muttered.

"Well, it felt like force, but it's fine, my muscles ache, and I don't know if I'm going to be able to move later, but it's no big deal. However, as I was saying, we gave you some time, and then you went off on that kid—though I probably would have done the same thing because he was a fucking idiot. But we're here now. You're going to tell us what's up."

"I don't know what's up. I didn't ask Sam any questions. I don't know why he's back. I didn't even know he was out of jail. They didn't tell me."

"The system doesn't really work all the time."

"I know that. I know it doesn't work. But it did get us Jack and Rose and each other. So, I can't really say that it sucks *all* the time."

Cameron nodded. "Yeah, Jack and Rose were the good ones. Sam wasn't. Our mother wasn't," Cameron said, gesturing between himself and Aiden.

I noticed Aiden stiffen just a bit, and I knew there was still tension there between the twins, between all of us when it came to Aiden, Cameron, and Dillon's birth mother, but we weren't going to get into that.

"I just don't know what to do," I said.

"Well, for all you know, he'll never come back again, and you won't have to deal with it at all." Aiden said the words quickly, and I looked up at him.

"You know life isn't that fair," I said, growling a bit.

"No, it's not. And even if Sam doesn't show up again, you'll still have to deal with your feelings about it. And I hate saying the word *feelings*, I feel like I'm going to grow a vagina at any moment."

"You're a dick," I said.

"Yeah, Rose probably would've slapped me upside the head for saying that." Aiden winced, and I just shook my head, laughing. It felt good to laugh, especially since, this time, it felt a little warmer than my cold ones from before.

"I don't know how I feel. Sam ruined everything. He was such an asshole. He was the worst of the worst. If he's not in jail and looked clean like he did, I don't know what he wants. But I have a feeling that won't be the last time I see him."

"Amends and all that shit," Dillon said from the doorway, and I looked up at him. "Sorry," the kid said. "I didn't mean to overhear anything, but I was coming back to see if you guys wanted food. I didn't realize you were already in the middle of your conversation."

I shook my head and gestured for him to come in. "No, come on in. You're our brother. If we ever have big issues where we have to vent to each other, you're part of it. And you're right about the amends. If Sam is clean, then he might be here to try and make amends."

"Fucking big ones," Aiden muttered.

"Truer words and all that shit," I said and then took a sip of my beer.

"I don't know what I'm going to do next. I think I'm past anger. I'm just sad. Or numb. Maybe I don't know what I need to feel, what I *could* feel."

"When Mom died, Cameron took me to this therapist who said I just needed to feel whatever I felt even if there wasn't a word for it. As long as I didn't hurt anyone or myself, it was fine. So maybe you need to do that," Dillon said, looking over at Cameron and then at me. "I wasn't very good at it at first, but then Cameron yelled at me, and I figured it out."

That made me laugh. "Cameron yelling helped you? I never would've thought."

"Douche," Cameron said, flipping me off.

And then we just sat there, laughing, talking about the fact that Rose and Jack probably would've slapped us all upside the head for using that type of language in the office—or anywhere near the bar that had once been our home.

It was nice just to let it all out, to make sure that the others knew I was okay even if I wasn't really okay. I didn't know what would happen next. I didn't know if I would see Sam again, but I had a feeling I would, and I would have to deal with it when the time came.

I just didn't know what I was going to say.

I helped out in the bar for a bit, then the others sent me home, knowing I wouldn't be much help, even on my day off. They all had things to do, and I had already done the paperwork. Plus, even though I didn't really want to be alone, I knew I needed sleep.

So, I sat down on my couch and just stared at my phone, wondering what to do and why I felt so lonely even though I had just been surrounded by people.

When I scrolled through my contacts, seeing without really seeing, I hovered over Harmony's name. But I didn't text her, didn't call her.

She had enough to deal with without my issues.

She had enough on her plate without me.

CHAPTER NINE

Sometimes I wonder if staying is too hard. Then I remember what I lost. What you gave me.

- Harmony to Moyer. 10 months ATE.

HARMONY

I LOOKED up at the big house that had brought me so many memories—stressful, loving, and a little worrying. That home had been the one to welcome me when I first met Moyer, even though I'd been so scared to meet my boyfriend's parents.

Because, at the time, that meant something serious. Meeting the parents was always serious.

And I hadn't really met many parents before I met Moyer's.

Yes, I had met a few when I was in high school, and even one set in college, but they hadn't been as serious because my relationships weren't as serious.

But then I met Moyer. And everything had changed.

So now, I was once again standing in front of the home Moyer had grown up in, the house he had stayed in for all his years until he moved out for school, then to live on his own, and then with me.

All of his early years had been spent here.

And some of my most cherished memories were from within in these walls—a holiday morning, a fire roaring with hot cocoa in our mugs.

Even mimosas after opening gifts.

We had alternated holidays, and it had been easy because both sets of our families lived in the same state.

His family had opened their arms to me even if I was wary at first. I hadn't known if they would like me. I hadn't known if I would be good enough for their child.

But they'd loved me, and it was weird. Not weird that they loved me, but in retrospect, maybe it was strange that we clung to each other as hard as we did after Moyer died.

Maybe some people would've taken a step back,

would've slowly walked away or even harshly shut that door so the memories didn't hurt as much.

But that wasn't something I ever wanted to do. It wasn't something Patrick and Kate wanted to do either.

So we had clung to each other, then given each other some space, and now we had become friends.

I was still their daughter-in-law, they were still my in-laws, but now, we were friends, as well. We did things together, and they hung out with my parents, too.

It was just...different.

Like *I* was different.

"Are you just going to stand out there and look at our house all day?" Kate asked, leaning against the doorway. She had her arms folded over her chest, her brows lifted. Her eyes danced.

Kate sometimes reminded me so much of Moyer that it startled me. Yes, Patrick was almost an older, mirror-image of Moyer but Kate had his smile and those eyes, and that's why Moyer's mother always reminded me of him.

Sometimes, it was hard to look into those eyes, knowing that Moyer wasn't here. Other times, it was a sweet memory.

It was harder to look at Patrick. To see the man Moyer would never become.

But then again, time did soothe wounds, even if not as quickly as I might've liked.

"Sorry," I called out, shaking my head, smiling. I walked up to the house and hugged Kate hard, sinking into her soft hold as Kate's arms went around me, clinging to me.

We hugged well, as if we were each other's lifelines. Though it wasn't like it had been right after, or even the year following.

Now, we were just two people with a shared past, and misery that didn't take up all of our lives anymore.

I didn't think others would understand that.

I didn't think that my friends actually understood why I still hung out with my in-laws sometimes. Maybe they thought I wasn't getting over my past, but getting over it wasn't really the reason I was moving on.

Moyer was my past, but his memory would always be a part of my present—and my future. And because I actually liked Kate and Patrick, I tended to *want* to spend time with them. Plus, it was good for us to remember Moyer, though we didn't put him at the forefront of our conversations or try to make it seem as if nothing had changed.

We were all growing, even if it might not make sense to an outsider. I told myself I wasn't just rationalizing that, even though it sometimes felt like it.

"Okay now, Harmony, let's get you inside. Patrick is manning the stove today since we're having stew. And you know him and his love for his stews. I made a set of pumpernickel rolls with a new recipe and, of course, Patrick taste-tested one just to make sure they were good enough for you."

Kate led me inside and helped me with my coat as she went on about the rolls and Patrick's stew. I loved the fact that they were both good cooks and each had their favorites. I never knew who was going to cook for me when I stopped by.

"Don't forget dessert," I said, grinning. "I didn't make the pie, sadly, but I got it from a bakery-slash-café downtown called Taboo. It's one of my favorite places to go for a snack or a sandwich."

Kate's eyes lit up as I handed over the pie I had set down on the bench when I first walked in. "Oh, it looks so yummy. Patrick and I keep meaning to go down there and visit the new shops and things, but we never find the time."

And it would probably be too hard for them to go near where Moyer had been killed. Kate didn't say that, but I understood. I'd forced myself to visit the place and try to keep up with my routine in the city even if it hurt more days than I wanted to count. But I was doing okay, something that I knew Kate and Patrick appreciated even if they might not understand all the time.

"Well, now I'm bringing Taboo to you. And the place

is right next to a tattoo shop if you're ever in the mood for ink." I winked, and Kate rolled her eyes.

"You know I hate needles."

"True, but you'd look good with a fairy on your shoulder." We walked into the kitchen as we talked, and she just shook her head.

"You and your friends can have all the ink you want. Me? I'm a little too chicken for that."

"Did I hear ink? Is my girl getting a tattoo?" Patrick asked as he walked to me, holding his arms out wide for a hug.

"Neither of us is getting a tattoo, Patrick," Kate said as she set down the pie on the kitchen island. "But Harmony did bring us pie from a little shop downtown. Kinky or something?"

I burst out laughing as Patrick met gazes with me, his brows waggling. "It's Taboo, Kate. Not Kinky."

"I don't know, kinky sounds kind of tasty," Patrick said before giving his blushing wife a kiss on the cheek.

"Paddy," she whispered and then pushed him away, still blushing.

I just shook my head, turning away slightly, grateful that the two were so loving with one another. They hadn't been for a while, each pulling away as they grieved their son, but now they seemed to be in a new phase. Not back to where they were because no one could really go back, but at least leaning on one another again.

"Okay, so we have pie, stew, and rolls," Patrick said, rubbing his stomach. "I think we're going to be very full and happy after dinner."

I nodded, agreeing. "Oh, yes." I moved over to look into the pot boiling away on the stove. "What kind of stew is this?"

"It's a pork stew. I know I usually go with beef or venison, but I figured pork would be a little bit like a treat for us. It's a different recipe, one that I haven't used before, but I tweaked it a bit."

He winked at me, and I just smiled. The man knew what he was doing when it came to soups and stews so I trusted him, even if I'd never actually had a pork stew before.

"I know I invited you over here for dinner, but remember I also said it was for something else?" Kate asked, a little hesitation in her voice.

I nodded, running my fingers over the marble countertop. I was a little worried about what she was going to say because sometimes our conversations weren't the easiest. But they weren't supposed to be. Not when what we'd gone through still sat between us.

"I remember. What can I do to help?"

Kate's eyes brightened for just a moment before her

face turned into a slight frown. "There are a few more boxes that we need to go through in the basement, and while Patrick and I could easily do it ourselves—no, *easy* is not the right word. We could do it ourselves, but we'd really like your help."

I swallowed hard and nodded. Sometimes, I felt like I was just numb enough that I could do things and have it not hurt.

Because I knew we were going through Moyer's things. He had lived here for a long time, it just made sense that there would be stuff here for him. Things that had been his.

"Of course, I'll help."

"If it's too hard, we won't. There's no rush. I just figured maybe we could go through a box every once in a while. Because I don't want to push him out, but I also don't want to feel like we're sinking into everything we once had and forgetting what we could have now."

I went over to Kate and hugged her tightly. "I know exactly what you mean. Don't worry. We'll get through this."

"And we'll have warm baked goods and stew and everything that's probably not the best for us once we're done," Patrick said, wrapping us both in his arms in a big group hug.

I followed them down to the basement and sat on a couch that they'd put down there.

They had renovated the space a few years ago, and Moyer had always wondered why they'd delayed so long. Apparently, they had waited to put in new bedrooms until they were ready for grandkids.

I ignored the little clutch in my belly, knowing that they wouldn't have any grandchildren in this house. Because even if I ever got married again, if I ever found a person I could actually trust and had children with them, Patrick and Kate wouldn't be their grandparents.

It was such an odd dichotomy, but it was something that others lived through daily. Something that I lived through daily. I didn't know how long Kate and Patrick would be in my life, but for now, they were. Regardless of what happened in the future, I hoped that we'd find a way to still connect. Maybe not as close as we were now, but we could still be family, even if titles were such a weird thing to have.

"Okay, I have two boxes. We can go through one or both. But they're from Moyer's college room. He stuck a bunch of his stuff in the back, and I forgot we had it."

"Oh, I didn't know he'd put stuff here from that late in life," I said, frowning and leaning forward a bit to look.

"He tended not to know what to do with certain things, so he gave them to us for safekeeping."

I nodded, remembering, and sank to the floor between Kate and Patrick. "That makes sense. I think Mom and Dad have a few things of mine, as well. Even though I have enough room for it now, I sort of like having a place in their home."

"Well, you're their baby, you'll always have a place there." Kate cleared her throat. "And a place here, too. Even when you're ready to move on and find a new part of your life, you'll always have a place here."

I swallowed hard, squeezing her shoulder before going to open the box. There really wasn't much to say to that, knowing that the words Kate said were absolutely true. We were all trying to figure out exactly how to move on, how to live this new life of ours, how to be in this new normal, even though we failed sometimes.

But sometimes, just sometimes, we did okay.

"Oh," I said, sucking in a breath. I looked down at the box, my hands going over some of the wrappings. "They're photos."

"Yeah," Kate said. "So many pictures. I sort of got in the habit of framing some of the ones he sent to us and then giving them back to him."

I smiled, looking down at one of the photos of Moyer smiling with a group of guys I didn't recognize. "This must be from high school."

"He was like that at home, too. He liked having photos

out but never got around to actually framing them himself."

"And then he found the app," Kate said, and the three of us laughed.

"I swear, the guy could've just printed them off on his computer and put them in frames himself, but he liked his app so much better," Patrick said.

I handed over the photo from high school and then picked up the next. My stomach clenched, and my hand shook as I brushed my fingertips softly against the young faces that stared back at me.

"I always liked our wedding photos," I said. "They weren't perfect. I had dark circles under my eyes since I'd had a headache and a stomach ache the night before and hadn't been able to really sleep. And Moyer had had one too many drinks, so he wasn't feeling well either. But in the end, it hadn't mattered, and our photos proved that."

I grinned, looking down at our young faces and then at Violet, Sienna, and Allison.

My heart lurched again as I stared down at Allison's sweet face. Her eyes were so happy. It looked as if she could face the world, and that nothing could ever come at her that she couldn't handle.

But that had been a lie.

Something had been hidden deep inside, and she'd lost her life because of it.

It wasn't easy to think about Allison. But then again, it wasn't easy to think about Moyer either.

Two bright lights in my life were now gone, and I was still here.

And, because of that, I'd learned that I needed to just breathe. And live.

Even if it wasn't always easy.

Tears fell as we looked down at more photos, some from when Moyer was in high school, others from college and after. It was like looking back at a past that I'd been a part of in some respects but not others. So many of these people had touched Moyer's life—some I had never met, and some I had known and cared for.

Kate had to leave the room at one point so she could wipe her face and blow her nose.

Patrick had watched her go as if not sure whether he should join her or let her be alone. In the end, he'd given her space and had given *me* a sad look.

We need to do this, needed to go through this. But I wasn't the same person I had been when I lost Moyer, and I was stronger for it.

Because I didn't try as hard. I didn't feel like I was losing part of myself as if I had lost a limb.

Instead, it was like looking back into memories and knowing that I had been happy.

That I could be happy again.

And that trust in fate, knowing that I could be happy without Moyer...sometimes that hurt more than anything.

But it was what he would've wanted. It's what I would've wished for him.

So, I was going to be happy.

Hence the dating and the girl-time and being with Brendon.

Because when I was with Brendon, he made me smile. He was just one of those friends that I could trust. Lean on.

And when I looked down at the selfie of him and Moyer smiling, one that Moyer'd had framed using his app, I frowned.

We were all so connected, the layers of friendships and relationships so convoluted that sometimes I forgot that Brendon had been so close to Moyer.

That I was close to them both.

I had known Brendon for longer than I had Moyer, and yet I had chosen Moyer. It was Moyer that I loved.

Moyer that I had married.

And now I looked at myself and thought about all the times I had talked to Brendon in the past few weeks. The fact that when I needed to talk, when things got to be too much, I called him.

I thought about the fact that we texted almost every

day, and we had lunches like we used to—only without someone between us.

Maybe I was leaning too much.

Because Brendon wasn't mine. He was a friend, yes, but maybe I was only friends with Brendon because I missed Moyer.

I rubbed my chest, thankful that Patrick and Kate weren't looking at me.

Now that I thought about it, it worried me that I was trying to lean on what I'd once had by connecting to a person who was a part of that past.

Yes, I was friends with the Connollys, and all of them were connected to Violet and Sienna, too.

But it was different with Brendon.

And that worried me.

Because I didn't want to hurt him, and I didn't want to be hurt again. I didn't want there to be a misunderstanding or, even worse, have me lean too much on him and end up hurting us both in the end.

I didn't know when Brendon had become the first person on my mind. I didn't know when that had begun.

And it worried me.

So I just went through the rest of Moyer's photos. Tears spilled down my in-laws' cheeks, but none ran down mine. I was numb once again, my mind in another place.

I took a couple of photos for myself, ones I didn't have, ones of groups of people rather than just Moyer.

But I didn't take any of Brendon.

I thought it would be weird to have him framed in my house when I was already so worried that I was leaning on him too much.

And then I ate dinner with Kate and Patrick, all of us smiling and laughing again. And, yes, we were all a little hurt inside, all of us stung a bit, but we were better than we had been before. We were human, healing, and just living.

By the time I got home, it was dark outside, and all I wanted to do was take a bath and maybe read a book. Perhaps drink a glass of wine—or five.

It was a little hard to think about exactly what was going through my head, especially since I was thinking about a little bit too much all at once.

Was I leaning on Brendon too much? I didn't think so, but maybe I was.

Because he was the one who I talked to about my dates. He was the one that, when I was stressed out, I called because I needed someone to talk to. Yes, I had the girls, and I called them often, but they were all dealing with so many of their own issues that sometimes I held back so they didn't have to worry about the widow anymore.

I was ashamed of that. Maybe I needed to step back and not put so much pressure on Brendon. I needed to not rely on him so much, or we'd end up hurting each other.

So, when I was in the tub, and my phone rang, I looked down and closed my eyes.

He was probably checking to see how I was doing. Because he knew where I had been. He knew that I had gone to have dinner with my in-laws and he likely wanted to make sure I was okay. I didn't want him to worry about me anymore, so I didn't answer. And when he texted, asking if I was okay and if he needed to come over, I picked up my phone and responded that I was fine.

Because I didn't want him to worry about me.

I didn't want him to have to see me as Moyer's widow anymore.

We might've slowly started reconnecting since Jack's death when Cameron had moved back to town, but I didn't want to get hurt, and I didn't want to hurt him.

So I didn't answer any more of his texts, and I didn't call back.

I just lay in the tub, wondering why I felt so off, why the numbness felt so different.

Because, once again, I wasn't the same Harmony I had been before.

I just didn't know who I was now.

CHAPTER TEN

BRENDON

"WHAT'S WRONG WITH YOU, BRENDON?" Violet asked, and I looked up at her. We were at Cameron's house after a decent lunch, and Violet had stayed after, staring at me. It had just been the brothers and Violet since none of the rest of us actually had women to bring.

It had been a little weird not having Harmony or Sienna with us, but then again, there were different layers of connections within the group now, something I was still getting used to.

"I'm fine," I said quickly, probably a little *too* quickly by the way her eyes narrowed on me.

"I don't actually believe you," Violet said, smiling.

"You don't really have to believe me. You just have to know that I'm saying things."

"That doesn't make any sense. Do you want to talk about it?"

"I'm not thinking about Sam, if that's what you're worried about," I said slowly. "I'm just thinking. I'm allowed to do that, you know."

"You are, and you're welcome to talk to us, too."

She leaned forward and squeezed my knee, and I smiled at her. Violet would one day be my sister-in-law. After all the time that Cameron and Violet had spent away from each other because of poor decisions—mostly on Cameron's part—they were finally together again.

Violet would be family, and that meant that Sienna and Harmony would be, too.

Because Harmony was their sister, if not by blood than by circumstance. Much as I was one of the Connolly brothers.

"I'm fine, I promise." Not quite a lie, but not the truth either.

"Do you want to talk about Sam? I mean, I know you did with the boys, but I'm a good listener. At least, sometimes."

"Not really. I haven't heard from him or seen him since he showed up, so I don't know where he's at. But I feel like he's just lurking, waiting to pounce at me when my guard's down."

"And that means you're never going to let your guard down," she said quickly. "Which sucks. That can't help with the whole stress of the situation."

"Not even a little. But it is what it is. I can only help my reactions and try not to focus on what the hell is happening with him. You know?"

"I know. But if you weren't thinking about Sam just then, what *were* you thinking about? It was as if you were staring off into the distance with a lot on your mind."

"Just everything, I guess. I haven't been sleeping. Work and the other work. And family. You know. Everything," I said, trying to sound casual. But I was anything but casual. Because all I could think about was Harmony. And the fact that she had just replied to my message with a text that she was fine and then hadn't contacted me again. Had I done something wrong? I knew I should have called or texted her when I went off the deep end at the gym and then tried to talk to my brothers. But I hadn't. Had she noticed? Was she trying to push me away like I was doing with her?

It didn't make any sense. I kind of hated myself for it.

Because it wasn't her fault that I was a little off-kilter, and I just wanted to make sure she was okay. She had told me that she was going over to Moyer's parents' house for dinner, and I was worried about her.

I always worried about her.

And, yeah, that was my problem. But now I was even more concerned that Harmony was pushing me away because I was acting weird. So...I just had to stop acting that way.

Easier said than done.

"Let's just go get a drink, shall we?" I said, looking directly into Violet's eyes.

I knew she was worried about me, but hell, it seemed like we were all worried about each other these days. Losing Jack and Rose had been hard, but we were pulling through. Almost losing the bar had been just as hard for some reason, as if we were losing another part of our past and our connections to each other.

But we were pulling through that.

And then Dillon joined the fold, making things a little more complicated, but the kid was good for us.

And now Cameron and Violet were back together, and that meant that Sienna and Harmony were back in our lives like they had been back in the day.

There was just so much going on that sometimes I worried I would get overwhelmed.

So, I wasn't going to worry about *any* of it.

Except for Harmony.

Her, I couldn't stop thinking about.

"If you say so. I could use a beer."

"Did someone say beer?" Cameron asked, holding three bottles in one hand.

"Ah, it's like you're reading our minds," I said, standing up. I reached out and took a bottle for myself and then Violet before handing hers over. "Is this one of the ones we're going to try for the bar?" I asked, looking at the label.

"Yeah, we're getting it next week in draft. But they're also bottling it in six-packs. And since I don't actually have a keg in the house, much to my dismay, I figured we could try the bottle, even though it's never quite as good, never the same."

Aiden and Dillon walked in behind Cameron, both holding beer bottles, as well.

"Hey, what's that in your hand?" I looked over at Dillon.

"Hey," he mimicked, "it's just a root beer." He lifted one hand, the other holding his bottle. "Seriously. Cameron said it's from the same company, so he got me some so I wouldn't feel all alone drinking milk."

I rolled my eyes, as it did indeed look like the kid was drinking a root beer. "Not a hard root beer, right?"

"No, I promise. I'm not going to fuck up. Believe me."

155

Cameron gave Dillon a hard look and then ruffled the kid's hair.

"Hey," Dillon shouted, ducking out of the way.

"Hey yourself. And you wouldn't like hard root beer. It's even more sickly sweet than the regular stuff in your hand right there."

"I like hard root beer. And hard cream soda. I'm not a huge fan of the hard grape. Mostly because I don't like grape anything." Violet just shrugged as we all turned to look at her. "What can I say, I also like Moscato and Sangria. I like sugar. Sue me."

"You know, sugar isn't good for migraines," Dillon said, and Violet just flipped him off.

Ah, family.

"I know sugar isn't good for migraines. So I don't have it often. But sometimes, I like it. And if I was going to stop having everything that was completely bad for me, I probably wouldn't have anything but water."

"You know, you're not wrong on that," I said and then lifted my beer. "To family lunches," I said, and we all clinked bottles.

I took a sip of the beer, nodding in appreciation as I looked over at Cameron. "Pretty good. A little hoppy for my taste, but I've never been a huge fan of all the IPAs that keep coming around."

"Why so many IPAs?" Aiden asked, throwing his head back as if he were exhausted at the mere thought.

"Because people like it. I know we all like ales more, and that's what we mostly have in the bar—ales, blondes, and pilsners. But we need IPAs because that's what people like."

"When did we get old?" Violet asked. "Because I feel like the younger generations of drinkers like IPAs more than the older generations. Am I old?"

I gave Aiden a look as both of us held back smiles, and Cameron quickly denied her question.

"It has nothing to do with age, baby. I promise." He leaned forward and kissed her lips, and Dillon rolled his eyes.

"So, does that mean I'm going to like IPAs?"

"You're not going to know until you're legal, boy," Cameron said. He reached over to ruffle Dillon's hair again, but the kid ducked out of the way.

"Hey, watch it with the hair. You're ruining my 'do."

"Your 'do?" I asked. "Okay, how old are you?"

"Oh, shut up."

"And Cameron, buddy," Aiden put in, "if you really think that this kid's not going to taste a sip of beer while he works in a bar with three brothers who actually own said bar, you're mistaken."

"I know the kid's going to drink beer."

"Hey, the *kid* is right here. You don't have to talk over me." Dillon looked between all of us, and I laughed.

"If you're going to have a drink, it won't be in our place. And you're not going to be stupid about it. There'll be no driving. No flashing anyone. There's no using drinking as an excuse to fuck around. You're going to be smart about it. And if you can wait until you're twenty-one, that would be great. But it would also be great if you could wait until you're married to have sex, and I know those things aren't going to happen."

The tips of Dillon's ears turned red, and Violet wrapped her arms around him. She smacked a loud kiss on his cheek and ruffled his hair.

"Violet," Dillon whined. He sounded much younger than the eighteen-year-old he was, and all of us couldn't help but laugh.

"Aw, my little baby brother."

"Violet," he whined again.

"What, you're just so cute. I can't wait to see you when you're all grown up and in a relationship. And definitely drinking beer."

"You know, I'm just going to start drinking wine," the kid growled, and we all chuckled.

"Wine is good. I like wine," Violet said. "And I bet you Harmony could figure out the best wine. Her family taught her everything they know about wines, and she's slowly starting to teach us. I mean, before I really started drinking, all I knew was that one was red and the other was white. I didn't even know what the pink one was."

"Harmony's family is in a little different type of society than we are," I explained to Dillon as he looked at us with a questioning glance.

"Oh, you mean she's rich?"

I rolled my eyes. "Yes, her parents are rich, and she has money herself." It had never bothered me before, even when I felt poor as hell in school. Now, I had money of my own, and Harmony was still the same person she'd always been.

"She seems classy. But not like the rich, snobby types that you see snapping their fingers at you or shaking the ice in their glasses when they want something. She's nice."

"Yeah, she is."

Violet gave me a weird look, and I quickly turned from her.

No one needed to know that I had feelings for Harmony. Feelings I really shouldn't have. It didn't matter that Moyer wasn't here anymore. She was my friend's girl, and there was no changing that. But that meant I needed to make sure she was okay. I needed to make sure *we* were okay. In doing so, I had to not be an asshole and put my problems on her doorstep.

We finished up our drinks, and while Dillon and

Aiden headed off to the bar, Cameron and Violet decided that it was time for a date even though they'd gone out on one the night before.

Apparently, new relationships meant a lot of dating. Who knew?

When I got into my car, I didn't head home like I probably should have. Instead, I took the next exit off the highway and found myself parked in front of Harmony's house.

This was probably a mistake. Then again, I was good at making those.

That's what happened when you fell for your best friend's widow.

It made you a letch.

But I had to push those thoughts from my mind and focus on the fact that Harmony was my friend, for better or worse.

Though not often worse.

I shook my head, pushing those thoughts away, and got out of the car. Not thinking about Harmony and trying to keep my distance only made the ache in my belly worse. So, I would work on being her friend.

I would just be there.

Because I didn't want to think about what would happen if I wasn't.

She answered the door just as I was about to ring the

doorbell. She had her auburn hair piled on top of her head, her face devoid of makeup and covered in specks of dust as if she'd been cleaning. Her cotton t-shirt hugged her breasts, and her curves were on display. I swallowed hard, trying not to look too closely.

She wore tight jeans with a hole in the knee that might have been made that way, and her feet were bare except for a little sliver of metal around a toe.

Why did she have such sexy toes?

And why was I still looking at her feet?

"Brendon?"

I looked up quickly into her face and swallowed hard. "Hey."

"I saw you pull up, so I figured I'd let you in before you rang the doorbell. What's wrong?"

I shook my head. "Nothing. I was just headed home from Cameron's and thought I'd stop by."

Neither of us mentioned the fact that her home was out of the way, but hopefully, she wasn't thinking about it.

A smile bloomed on her face. "Come on in. I'm just cleaning cabinets as you can tell from the amount of dust I probably have on my face."

She grinned as she took a step back, and I walked in behind her. Before I could think better of it, I reached out and used my thumb to wipe some of the dust from her cheek.

She blinked, her pupils dilating just a fraction, and I wondered what that meant. She looked a bit startled at the contact but smiled even wider. "That bad, huh?"

I quickly took my hand away, knowing I'd remember the warmth I felt until the end of my days, even if it made me a bastard.

"You look beautiful, Harmony. As always."

She tilted her head, studying my face. "You're good for my ego. I should keep you around."

"Yeah, maybe you should."

And that was the crux of it, wasn't it?

Because I wanted to stay. Even if I shouldn't.

CHAPTER ELEVEN

Remember when Allison asked if you had brothers?
You were perfect for me.

And I'm so sad that I never found someone
perfect for her.

- Harmony to Moyer. 22 months ATE.

HARMONY

I HADN'T SLEPT well the night before. And it was odd for me since I'd been sleeping well until recently.

I'd had another dream about Allison, and after I'd

woken up, shaking just slightly, I couldn't go back to sleep. After tossing and turning, I'd lain there for hours, wondering if maybe I shouldn't have gone to sleep at all the night before, not with so much going on in my mind. Because sometimes it was harder than others to remember that life needed to move on, something that I'd told myself over and over again for the past two years.

But between losing Allison what felt like hours ago instead of months, and then trying to date again, sometimes my emotions were a little off-kilter. That's why I was glad I was going to have a girls' day today. Every time the ladies and I were together now, we tried to live in the moment, even if the moment wasn't good.

Because Allison had been our good. And we had lost her far too soon to demons none of us had seen. And that was something we all had to live with.

But in order to do that, we had to live. So, we got together often. We were each other's family. And we made sure that we remembered her even as we tried to find a new path. I had taken this road before, even if it was far different.

I didn't like that I had a roadmap for grief, but maybe it was the only way I could keep going. Perhaps it was the only way I could still be me.

Right now, though, it wasn't necessarily about that.

Right now was about my friends and the way that we were going to be together.

Between work and using my free time to go on perpetually worse blind dates, I hadn't spent as much time with just the girls as I had in the past.

I missed them.

I missed just hanging out, maybe doing a spa day if we felt like it, but really, I just missed having wine and sitting down and talking.

Just being.

It had been too long since we had just been ourselves: the girls.

Women.

So, today was going to be about that.

And they were all coming to my house rather than us going to Violet's or Sienna's or even Meadow's now that she was joining us. It was my turn, and that meant I had to have the best charcuterie board, the best wine, and other snacks for them.

Okay, maybe not the best, but I liked making sure they felt special. I enjoyed making sure that no one wanted for anything.

It wasn't about flashing money, it wasn't about having the actual best things in the world. It was about showing that I appreciated my friends and that I loved them.

I hummed as I worked in the kitchen and smiled as the doorbell rang.

I set down my cheese knife, wiped my hands on a towel, and went to open the door, smiling at Violet and Sienna who stood on the doorstep, chocolate in hand.

"I know you always have everything, as do all of us when we host, but I found chocolate that I like and I wanted to share." Violet winked as she walked in, giving me a hug and handing over the box of chocolates.

I looked down, my mouth watering. "Oh, is this that new chocolatier downtown?"

"Yes," Sienna said, kissing me on the cheek as she gave me a hug. "It's a place I really wanted to try, even though I haven't had a lot of time to go. So, we're going to eat some chocolate and whatever amazing food you have for us and drink wine. A lot of wine for me, since Violet is the designated driver for the two of us."

I shook my head and set the chocolates on the entryway table. "Really? You're going to get completely drunk?"

"I just might."

"I'm still getting over my last migraine, so I probably won't be getting too tipsy," Violet said. "Plus, you know, the whole driving thing."

"You're always welcome to just stay here tonight, or

call one of the guys if you don't want to limit yourself to just one glass of wine."

"They are all working tonight since they're doing another wing night."

I nodded, tapping the bridge of my nose. "I forgot. Brendon said they were going to try a wing and tapas night or something like that. He had an actual name for it. I can't remember, but it sounded better than wings and tapas."

"Yeah, it's not actually a wing night," Violet said, laughing. "Not if Aiden has anything to say about it."

"Aiden is determined to make the place upscale."

I gave Violet a look as Sienna growled at herself over Aiden.

I had no idea what was going on between the two of them, considering they kept fighting with each other even though they'd always been closer friends than I remembered. But, people changed, and some things just happened. It would have been nice if they'd told me what was going on, but it wasn't my place to actually know everything about all of my friends.

I was just about to ask if they knew when Meadow was going to arrive when the doorbell rang.

"And there's our fourth," I said and then froze.

We all looked at each other, our eyes wide, Violet's a little teary. Because Meadow wasn't our fourth. More like our fifth. And five was a great number. There was nothing wrong with five.

But our fourth wasn't here anymore.

I smiled and hoped it reached my eyes because I didn't want Meadow to feel like she was anything less.

Because there was nothing less about the woman who was so quiet and reserved that I knew she held herself back.

But Meadow also took care of Violet when Violet couldn't take care of herself. And for that, I would be forever grateful.

I didn't say anything to the other girls as I opened the door and smiled at Meadow.

"You're here," I said, knowing my voice might sound a little shaky, but it was the best I could do.

Meadow met my gaze, and I knew right then that she had heard the tremor. That hesitancy.

And I felt horrible.

"You told me not to bring anything, but I did bring goat cheese. I know, it sounds weird, but I went to a farmer's market recently and actually met the goat that made this cheese, and it made me happy. So, I brought a little bit. You can either keep it for later or use a little bit tonight."

I opened my arms and hugged Meadow tightly, relaxing ever so slightly. It was hard not to relax or feel a little protective when it came to Meadow. There was just something about her.

"Thank you. I'm in the middle of my charcuterie board preparation, and I think I have the perfect spot for it right behind the grapes and next to the Goldfish crackers."

Meadow blinked. "Goldfish crackers?"

I just laughed. "One of my friends online started putting Goldfish crackers on her board because of her little girl, and it became a thing. So, no charcuterie board, no matter how gorgeous, is complete without at least a few Goldfish crackers."

"Well, I love them, so I guess that sounds just fine for me."

I helped them all with their coats, and Violet went and opened a bottle of wine.

We were a mix of red tonight, so there was a second bottle open, and then all of us were sitting in the kitchen, making final preparations.

"Everything you have is just so lovely," Meadow said. "As if it's cared for yet sparkly and pretty at the same time."

A blush ran across the other woman's cheeks, and I just laughed.

"I like pretty things. I always have. This is my first real home of my own." Violet and Sienna just nodded along, and Meadow looked as if she had said something wrong.

"No, really. I'm okay. I went from living with my parents to the dorm to living in a small apartment because I hadn't wanted to use my trust fund yet. I wanted to work hard to actually pay for my first home rather than use the money that had been given to me."

"That's why I love you," Violet sing-songed, the light in her eyes dancing, the mistiness gone.

"Anyway, after that, I moved in with Moyer, and the place was ours. So, there was a little masculine feel to it, a little feminine, but it was very much a married couple's feel where everything is slightly compromised yet not. This place, though...this place is mine. So, yes, there's a little more sparkle because I love chandeliers."

"And it's not like the lighting is gaudy or anything," Sienna said, rolling her eyes.

"No, nothing gaudy. Just subtly pretty."

"And you even have a charcuterie board with handles. I mean, really, how amazing is that?" Violet said, holding up the board for all of us to see.

"That I got at Target."

"Oh, yes, Target. The devil's lair," Meadow said, and we all laughed.

"Yeah, I can't actually walk into that place without spending way more than I planned." I shook my head and laughed. "And I know it's like that for everybody. But how can you walk in there and not accidentally buy eighteen things you don't need?"

"I'm like that at the grocery store," Sienna said. "I'll have a list and make sure I don't go down every aisle just in case I accidentally get things I don't need, but I still end up with like fifteen things I didn't plan on."

"Subliminal advertising at its best," I said and then took a bite of a carrot. "Now, we have our cheese and charcuterie. We have some bread that I freshly baked this morning."

"You baked bread?" Violet said, her voice deadpan. "Well, aren't you just Martha Stewart all of a sudden? Okay, not so all of a sudden since you're always Martha, but now a little more so with the bread and the like."

"I used a bread maker rather than the oven because I wasn't going to actually deal with kneading myself."

"Ah, that makes me happy."

"Anyway, it's a honey white bread, so it's horribly bad for you. And I don't care. I also made a few other appetizers including things with bacon because bacon is life, and we have some wine. And water for when you're done with your single or several glasses, depending on what you want tonight. But we have food, wine, and great company." I held up my glass of red in a toast, and the others did the same. "To friends. To new friends, to old friends, and everything in between. Thanks for being here with me. Just, thanks."

My eyes filled with tears just a little as the others toasted my glass, their eyes watery, as well.

"Okay, enough of that, let's talk about dates," Sienna said, her eyes bright. "Because I don't need to get mushy right now, I don't want my mascara to run."

"You're using the wrong mascara then," I said sagely. Sienna just shrugged. "Maybe, but anyway, I want to hear about your latest date."

I sighed, leaning against the counter. "You really don't."

"It couldn't have been worse than the first two," Violet said, leaning forward. "Because those were not good."

"You've been on three blind dates?" Meadow asked, and I nodded.

"Yes, three blind dates that three so-called friends set me up on."

"None of us set you up with those people. Just reminding you," Violet said, her voice stern.

"No, because I don't actually want my best friends setting me up with people just in case it's in their circles, and things get weird. I'm not very good at this dating thing." I rubbed my chest over my heart, wincing. "I wasn't even good before Moyer. I kind of just fell into a relationship with him, and it turned out we actually liked each other and then loved each other. I'm really not good at the whole finding-my-own-date thing, apparently."

"I'm not good at dating either," Meadow said. "In fact, I'm pretty terrible at it."

"I'm not any better," Sienna said, taking a big gulp of her wine. "In fact, I could probably write a story about how bad I am at dating."

"Well, I am one lucky bitch," Violet said, sipping her wine daintily. "I mean, I even had sex before I came here. After a lunch date with my man. I guess I really am a lucky bitch."

Violet ducked the snap pea coming her way from sweet Meadow's direction. I just laughed.

"No throwing food in my kitchen, young lady," I said, even though I was laughing. Meadow just smiled sweetly. "I have no idea what you're talking about. The snap pea just flew at her on its own, as if it couldn't stand any more bragging."

"Okay, the snap pea did have its reasons," I said, laughing.

"You guys are just mean. Plain mean." Violet picked up the snap pea and tossed it in the trash.

"Anyway, now that we're done making sure Violet is the most hated person in the room, tell us about your date."

"Well, it wasn't great," I said simply.

"You said that already. How not great was it?" Sienna asked.

"Well, his name was Dirk."

That made Violet snicker. "Dirk? Really?"

"Hey, I've known a nice Dirk in my life," Meadow said. And then she winced. "Of course, he ended up being an asshole in the end, but just like any man, and any name, there are good ones."

"Anyway, Dirk was a nice guy. He was another friend of a friend of Candace's. I'm not going to hold that against her though because they didn't really know each other. Candace knew Dirk's ex-girlfriend."

All the girls winced at that, and Violet held up her wine glass in a toast. "Ah."

"Ah, indeed. Anyway, he talked about his ex, Debbie, the entire time."

"Dirk and Debbie?" Sienna asked, grinning. "That's actually kind of sweet."

"I think so, too. And Debbie sounded like a wonderful woman."

"Oh, so he wasn't talking bad about her?" Violet asked.

"Not in the slightest. If I didn't know that Debbie was an actual real woman, I would have thought she was the epitome of angelic grace. I don't think that woman could do wrong in his eyes."

"That might have been the problem," Meadow said.

"Yeah, you're right about that. Because I really do think that Dirk is in love with Debbie. He talked about the way she cared for animals and how she was so sweet, and how he felt like he couldn't do enough to make sure she knew that he loved her. But he also didn't want to be too scary about it because of the fact that they had met through an app."

"Dating's rough," Sienna said.

"Yeah, very rough. And I haven't even started app dating."

"Run. Run far away from that," Meadow said. I looked at her.

"Tried it before?"

"Once. Never again." Meadow visibly shuddered, and I nodded.

"Yeah, anyway, I really hope that Dirk calls Debbie because there was genuine love in his voice when he spoke about her. And not like the obsessive, crazy love. But how he was just happy that he got to spend time with her. And I could tell that he'd walked away because she asked him to, and he didn't obsess. Didn't push. Just wanted her to be happy. I hope that she loves him just a fraction of what he obviously feels for her. Because that was true beauty."

"And you learned all of this on your date with him," Sienna said drily.

"Yep. But, it's fine. We had a nice date as friends. And he has my number so he can tell me exactly when he gets back together with Debbie. Because I feel like it's going to happen."

"It might not happen if she doesn't want it. And I hope he doesn't push her," Meadow said. There was something in her voice that worried me. But I didn't push, because tonight wasn't the night for that, and I didn't think Meadow was ready.

"I only say that because Debbie called him at the end of our date."

"Oh," Sienna said. "Interesting."

"And you should have seen the way Dirk's eyes lit up. Like it was true love. Something I hope others could see in Moyer's eyes when he thought of me. You know?"

Meadow reached out and gripped my hand. "I know."

I gave her fingers a squeeze before letting go.

"Anyway, he left because Debbie said she wanted to talk, and I was so happy for him that I didn't even mind that he walked out on our date to go meet with his ex."

"I swear, you have the weirdest dates. But dating is weird, so maybe not." Sienna just shook her head. "Remember when Allison went on that date with that guy who wanted to be a zoologist, but really he just wanted to stare at animals?"

"Oh, God," Violet said, shuddering. "Don't bring up Zeke the freak."

I laughed, wiping tears from my face. "His name was not Zeke. It was Zack."

"Yes, but Zack and freak didn't sound good together, so he was always Zeke the freak to us. Allison even painted a picture of Zeke the freak. And not an animal in sight. Those poor babies."

"Allison really had poor taste in men." I paused. "Except for Aiden. She and Aiden were a good match. At least when they were younger."

We all went silent for a moment, and I couldn't help but notice the way Sienna took a big gulp of her wine then looked down at her empty wine glass.

We were all hurting, and yet we were bringing up people who we had lost over time. It was healthy.

But even after all of the talk, it just reminded me that maybe I really wasn't ready for dating. I just wasn't any good at it.

We moved our food and wine into the living room and turned on a rom-com that we didn't really watch, we just mostly talked to each other about nothing and everything.

Violet and Meadow had both switched to water, and Sienna had slowed down, now only on her third glass of wine. I was on glass number two but was probably going to call it a night for the alcohol soon. We all had plans the next day, after all.

We were just talking about the next pool tournament and if we were going to enter when my phone buzzed. I looked down at it and smiled.

Brendon: *Drunk yet? Or just full of cheese?*

Me: *Just happy...and full of cheese.*

Brendon: *Aiden made these stuffed fig things tonight with goat cheese and I think I fell in love with a goat.*

Me: *Remind me to tell you about Zeke the freak.*

Brendon: *I'm scared.*

Me: *You should be.*

"Who has you smiling like that over there?" Violet asked, sounding curious.

"Oh, just Brendon, making sure I'm doing okay tonight." I blinked and set my phone down on my lap.

"Ooh," Violet and Sienna said together as they looked at me.

I waved them off, feeling the heat creep to my cheeks. Why was I blushing? It was only Brendon. "Oh, shut up. He's just checking on me. You know Brendon."

"Brendon doesn't check on *me* like that," Sienna said, leaning forward to look over my shoulder at my phone.

I hid the screen, not knowing why. Brendon was just my friend. There was no reason that anyone who wanted to couldn't look at my screen. But for some reason, I wanted it to just be mine. I wanted his words to be mine.

And I had no idea what that meant, nor did I know what the warm feeling inside of me suggested.

"Give me a second so he doesn't worry," I said quickly.

"Ok-ay," Violet said as the others gave each other looks I purposely ignored.

Me: *Have a good night tonight. Just don't mess with Beckham by pretending to bartend.*

Brendon: *I'm insulted.*

Me: *No, you're not. You can pour me wine anytime. Just don't make me a martini.*

Brendon: *That's fine. Next time it's a double.*

Me: *The horror!*

Brendon: *You're a riot.*

Me: *I try.*

Brendon: *Sure, honey.*

Me: *Go work. I'm going to have more wine and cheese. Because I need it. Night-night, Brendon.*

Brendon: *Night, Harms.*

A smile played on my face, and I couldn't help but notice the way the others looked at each other, giving one another strange looks that weren't so secret.

They could think what they wanted to, but Brendon

was my friend. I had tried to push him away for our own good because I thought I was leaning on him too much, but then I realized as soon as I saw him next, as soon as I spoke to him, that it was a stupid thing to do.

I was just scared.

So scared.

Though I didn't know why.

And maybe I should think about that. Perhaps I should think about that warm feeling inside.

Instead, I set down my phone and went back to talking with my friends. Brendon would be there later. And then I would think about exactly what was going on inside my head.

CHAPTER TWELVE

BRENDON

"YOU'RE GOING TO DIE, MOTHERFUCKER," Dillon shouted, and I pinched the bridge of my nose.

"Language."

"You're starting to sound like that Captain America GIF," Dillon grumbled. "Plus, I'm over eighteen. Kind of allowed to curse."

"You kind of cursed like a sailor before you were eighteen, too," Cameron said, shaking his head. "And...take that, motherfucker," he added, pressing a button on his controller.

I laughed as Dillon stood up, cursing even worse than before, though being respectful about it at the same time.

The brothers were over for a video game battle, though we were doing it quite early in the morning rather than later in the afternoon or even in the evening like most people. We were in the food service and bar industry. That meant our hours were weird.

We'd even somehow gotten Beckham to join us today. Which was kind of nice because Beckham was a stealth fighter when it came to playing video games, and that meant Cameron and Dillon didn't win every time. They usually did, but beggars couldn't be choosers.

Aiden and I weren't the best at playing video games, though we held our own. Somehow, Violet and Sienna were better than we were, even though they hadn't played when they were younger and hadn't logged the hours.

But, apparently, their older brother Mace had taught them well, even from afar, and they could kick our asses.

It wasn't that they were girls or that girls couldn't play, it was more the whole practice thing. I had dedicated my life to video games as a middle-schooler and teenager. That had been the first thing I leaned on once I finally realized that I was allowed to actually be a Connolly and not live in the past as much as I had.

And yet I still wasn't very good at it.

Dillon and Cameron were like fucking savants.

I didn't know if Harmony could play. She hadn't played with us when we were younger, and it wasn't like she played with us now. I only knew that Violet and Sienna could still play because we'd played one night at Cameron's house when Harmony wasn't there.

Now, I was thinking about Harmony again, even though I shouldn't. But I could tell myself that I shouldn't do a lot of things. It didn't mean I would stop thinking about them.

After all, Harmony haunted my nightmares. She infused so many parts of me.

I knew I needed to do something about it. Either cleanse her from myself or tell her how I felt.

Because I couldn't keep going, couldn't ignore the matter anymore. And I couldn't stop this aching feeling from entering my gut whenever I thought about her.

It wasn't her fault that I was falling for her. Wasn't her fault that I loved her.

Loved.

Holy shit.

I loved Harmony.

How did that happen?

But then I really thought about it. I thought about how I love the way she smiled. The way she leaned in whenever someone spoke to her as if she were truly hearing them, truly understanding. Really wanting to be part of the conversation.

Everything about Harmony was sincere. Yes, sometimes, she had to put on airs, but only when someone made her uncomfortable. Still, she was there, present.

She had pulled herself from the ashes not once but twice and was stronger for it.

I was in awe of her. Of her beauty, her grace, her intelligence. And I might've thought the word *beauty* first, but it wasn't the first thing about her that made me want her.

I had always been drawn to her, but first only as a friend. Even when we were younger, even before Moyer, I had known that I wanted to be in Harmony's life.

But it wasn't until after, until she was back in my life, that something had clicked inside me.

And I've never felt so much guilt.

Because Harmony wasn't mine. She couldn't be. She *shouldn't* be.

She was Moyer's. And even if she was going on all these dates, ones that weren't working out for her but still made me want to throw up, I had no claim to her.

I couldn't be jealous. I couldn't wish for those dates to go badly. Because I wanted the best for her.

And I didn't think I could be the best.

Because I was a kid from the streets, one who'd lived in filth, who had been sold for drugs. Who had done things I never wanted to talk about again. Things that I only spoke about with my therapist if needed. But never again.

It didn't matter that I'd had to go back to therapy, didn't matter that I was trying to get through it all, or that I still needed to be clean. It didn't matter that Sam was back, at least in the city. He wasn't in my life, but he was back. None of that mattered because I wasn't for Harmony.

"You want to tell me what's on your mind?" Beckham asked as he strolled into the room.

I looked over at the man and shook my head. "Not really sure what there is to say."

"Well that's a crock of shit," Aiden said, taking a sip of his tea. "I mean, we all know you're thinking about her. So why don't you fucking do something about it?"

"Just stop it. You've no idea what you're talking about."

"Didn't even have to say her name, and yet you knew exactly who I was talking about," Aiden said knowingly. "What does that say to you? Who am I talking about, big brother?" Aiden asked, leaning forward.

Cameron and Dillon had turned off the game, and everybody stood up to look at me.

I hated being the center of attention. I felt as if I were throwing dirt on myself just by having them watch me. I knew it was all psychological and that I was fine, I was clean, had just showered that morning after all, but it was like something itched under my skin, and I just wanted people to stop looking at me.

"Breathe, Brendon. You're fine. Okay?" I looked at Cameron and nodded. Then I looked at Aiden, who gave me a quick once-over before moving his gaze away.

The twins knew my issues with cleanliness. They knew how I liked wearing suits because it made me feel a little more dressed, and a little further from the kid I had once been. We all had issues, quirks, and that was mine.

Dillon and Beckham had probably figured it out after the number of times I washed my hands. But it was fine, I was dealing with it. I had a therapist. I had medicine. I was fine.

But none of that had anything to do with the fact that I couldn't think about Harmony anymore. I couldn't.

"We're talking about Harmony, right?" Dillon asked, looking between all of us. I let out a laugh.

Everybody started chuckling, and it was like the vacuum had burst, a bubble popping. Tension slid out of the room, even if a new type burbled beneath the surface.

"Yeah, kid, we're talking about Harmony," Beckham said. I looked sharply at the other man.

"You, too?"

"Hey, I'm a bartender. Another form of therapist, if you will."

"So, what? You see all and know all?" I asked sarcastically.

"Yep. Still a better bartender than you." He winked, grinning under his beard for a moment before going back to his normal look of detachment.

I flipped him off and laughed, needing that.

"Yes, okay? It's about Harmony. Can't be about Harmony. But it is. That's who I was thinking about. Can we just stop talking about it?"

"You're the one who keeps saying her name," Cameron said, stuffing his hands into his jeans' pockets. "But we've been very good about not questioning you about it."

"Yeah, we just talk about it behind your back," Aiden said, grinning.

I flipped him off, too. For good measure. "Seriously? You guys talk about this? What are you guys saying? I don't even know what I'm thinking, and yet you think you can just talk about it as if you guys know more than I do?" I was starting to raise my voice, so I slid my hand through my hair and then started pacing. "I have no idea what the fuck I'm doing. I can't have this feeling. I can't have any feeling when it comes to her. We're just friends. Friends."

"And if you keep telling yourself that, maybe one day you'll believe it," Cameron said. "Brendon. She's single.

You're single. I see the way you look at her. It's not just the fact that you think she's hot." A pause. "Because she *is* hot."

"Hey, you're dating Violet. Eyes off." I snapped out the words, and all four sets of brows rose. Great. Now, who was being a territorial asshole? It was one thing I really didn't want to do.

"Yes, I am dating Violet. She's the love of my life, and one day I'm going to marry her. I also think that her friends are hot. I'm a man. I have eyes. It happens. But that does not mean I'm going to actually move on any of those feelings. You, on the other hand, have more feelings than that. We all know it."

"Oh? And what exactly am I feeling? Because I don't even really know yet." That was a lie, considering I'd just told myself that I loved her, but I wasn't going to say that out loud. I could barely think about it without wanting to throw up, so that meant I wasn't going to say the words to anyone else.

Let alone Harmony.

Oh, God, there was that bile again.

"I think you need to talk with her," Dillon said.

I looked at the kid, shaking my head. "You have no idea what you're talking about, Dillon. There's a lot more than just what you see on the surface. A whole lot more."

"I know things."

"Dillon."

"I do, I know that she used to be married to your friend from work. I know that Moyer died. I know that Allison died recently and that's adding a whole new layer of issues to her already somewhat healed grief. I know she's going on dates because everyone keeps talking about how bad they are. I know that she talks to you after almost every one. Am I right? Yeah, I think I'm right. So, after every bad date, she ends up talking to you and her friends to feel better. What do you think that means? And don't say you're in the friend zone. Friend-zoned is just something that gets brought up to make everyone think that because they're in the friend zone, they have the right to make everyone feel bad about it instead of feeling like they're allowed to feel. Meaning, whatever they *want* to feel."

My head spun.

"You lost me there," I said, rubbing my temples.

"I'll get back to Harmony in a minute. Friend-zoned is what some guys think they're put in when a girl doesn't want them, and they're just friends. That is just called being a friend. It's not a weigh-station for them to think you're hot so you can get in their pants. Friend-zoned is just a stupid, stupid thing that I hate. However, I'm off-topic. You and Harmony look at each other."

"Before we talk about that last sentence," Cameron

interrupted, "I've never been prouder of you, Dillon. I'm just going to put that out there."

My head whirled. I felt like I was two steps behind on this conversation. At least with respect to women. However, I was still lost.

"What do you mean we look at each other? We're friends. You know that."

"No," Dillon said softly. "You *look* at each other," he repeated, emphasizing the word. "You see each other. You're friends, sure, but it's like you guys have inside jokes that you didn't even know you had. You always rely on each other, and you always team up, no matter what. That's not just being friends. You have a solid foundation. And I know that if you're this stressed out, whatever you're feeling for her is important. It's real. So, maybe you need to do something about it."

"And what if I do something about it?" I asked the room. "What if I go and tell her that I want something more. That I don't want to just be her friend. What if I tell her and everything gets fucked up? What are we going to do then? Because it's not just her and me anymore. It's all of us. We're a group."

"We're a group," Aiden agreed. "But that's not all of it. No matter what our dynamics are as a unit, if we start dating within it, we'll figure out how to deal with that.

We're figuring out a way to remain together without Allison. Without our parents. We added Dillon." Aiden gestured to the kid. "Hell, we're adding Beckham and Meadow, too. The group can change, it has multi-layered dynamics. But that is not what is worrying you. At least it's not the main thing."

I looked at all of them, swallowing hard.

"And?"

"And it's not your dad," Beckham said softly, and I looked over at the other man.

"Excuse me?"

"Hey, don't get mad at me. I might not know everything about your past, but I remember seeing the man that walked into the bar. I know what a former addict looks like. Believe me. And I know the three of you are foster kids that went through fucking hell before you came to Jack and Rose. I don't need to know the details. If you want to tell me, I'm here. And not just because I'm your bartender. Because I'm your friend. I know you went through hell. And I know you're not that kid anymore. And I have a feeling that seeing that man come into the brewery probably rattled your cage some. But that's not why you're worried about Harmony. Not the biggest part."

"You don't think I know I'm not good enough for her?

Because I know that. I might wear a suit, I might be a completely different person than I was when I was living on the streets, but she's high-class, and I was street. I was trash." A little out of breath, I added, "A little sheen's not going to change that."

"You're lucky I don't punch the shit out of you," Aiden snapped. "A little sheen? Fuck that. Jack and Rose didn't give you a little *sheen*. They gave you a family. Yeah, we fucked that up before. We all walked away when we shouldn't have. But we're back together again. And there's four of us now. Five if you include Beckham, but I don't think he really wants to be a Connolly."

"Thanks," Beckham added dryly.

Aiden shook his head. "Jack and Rose did not give you a little sheen," he repeated. "They gave you a family. They gave you support. You're not that kid anymore. Yeah, maybe he's somewhere deep inside, and hell, all our little kids are still inside us, fucking us over every once in a while with who we used to be. But you have a lot more history than those years you lived on the streets. And I think that past is what's standing in your way."

I looked at all of them, and then down at my hands.

I had no idea how we had gotten here. All five of us standing in my fucking living room trying not to talk about the important things and yet only talking about them.

"Moyer's gone," Cameron said softly. "He's gone, and he's not coming back. But look at her, Brendon. Look at the way she survived."

I looked up at my family, my friend, and shook my head. Tears stung my eyes, but I didn't let them fall. This wasn't the time to break down. I was already ragged inside. "I know she survived. She's so damn strong. So fucking amazing." I took a deep breath. "I know that Harmony isn't mine. She can't be. Can she?"

"At least you're asking the right questions now," Dillon added. "I mean, she's out there dating, and she's still smiling. And she talks about him. The fact that I even know his name means it's not something we don't talk about because it hurts too much. Losing people you love is going to hurt, but being able to talk about them is a way of healing. And you're part of that. You knew them both. And if she wants nothing to do with you, I know you won't force her to date you or some crap like that. But it's not fair for you to hold it all inside."

"Where the hell did you learn all this?" Cameron asked. "Because I'm not that good at parenting."

Dillon looked up at him and shrugged, stuffing his hands into his pockets just like Cameron had done before. "You're not that bad. And I hear things. I learn things. I guess. And TV helps."

I snorted, shaking my head. "I don't know what to do."

"Then you need to think about it." I looked over at Aiden when he spoke. "Either you don't do anything about what you're feeling, and you pine. Or you continue not doing anything, and you find someone else to date. Maybe that'll help. Maybe that will let you get through this so you can let her live her life, and you can live yours. Or, maybe, you do something else about it. Because standing back and watching your life pass you by without actually living it? That's not something that Jack and Rose ever wanted us to do. I see the way she looks at you, even if she doesn't realize she's doing it. You two have a connection. Maybe you should try and do something about it."

Bile rose in my throat again, and I just shook my head. "I don't know. I don't know what to do."

"Then at least try to be honest with yourself," Cameron said.

"And then you can be honest with her. As long as you know the words first, you can find them to tell her." At Beckham's words, the others seemed to realize that I needed a moment alone, so they gathered their gear, said goodbye, and left me alone in my house with my thoughts and whatever the fuck I was feeling.

I looked down at my hands and wondered if I was making a mistake.

Of course, maybe the mistake was me standing here not doing anything about what I felt.

Maybe I just needed to stop acting like a dick and actually bare my heart to her. Or, at least surrender a part of it.

Because standing in the wings, watching Harmony live her life and wondering how I could be a part of it wasn't healthy.

It wasn't fair to either of us.

I knew I'd been coming to this moment for far longer than just the minutes I had with my friend and brothers talking about it.

I needed to do something about it.

I had to.

And so, I somehow found myself in my car, driving to Harmony's house, hoping she would be there. I didn't know her work schedule by heart or if she'd be out with her friends.

I didn't text her ahead of time, I didn't call her. I didn't do anything but get in my car and have it take me to her.

Because everything I'd done up to this moment had been leading me to her.

Even if I went through the motions, even if I told myself that I wasn't good enough for her, even if my past wasn't perfect, I couldn't hold back any longer.

And what scared me most, more than I cared to admit, was that she saw Moyer when she looked at me.

I had no idea what I would do if that were the case. I had no idea what I would do if that were the only thing she saw.

But I didn't know if I could go on without telling her how I felt. Without having her in my life.

I was going to risk everything.

I might end up breaking everything in the end for a woman I shouldn't have, one I shouldn't want.

But the others had said that she looked at me, and I wanted to believe that. I wanted it to be true so much that I was going to risk everything just to tell her how I felt. To let her know what I wanted, even if I didn't exactly know what that was.

"Okay, come on, you can do this," I whispered to myself as I pulled into the driveway. Thankfully, I saw Harmony's car there, and I turned off my own engine, wondering if I would be able to get out of the vehicle at all.

And then I was on my feet, the car door closed behind me. I didn't even remember getting out.

Maybe that was good. Because if I thought too hard, I would probably just throw up.

And vomiting on her rose bushes probably wasn't the best way to tell her that I had feelings for her.

So, I knocked on the door and waited.

And waited.

And waited.

She didn't answer.

I didn't know what else to do, and then I just laughed. I shook my head. It figured she wouldn't be there. The one time that I actually had enough balls to do something about what I felt, and she wasn't there.

I snorted, turned on my heel, and made my way back to my car. Maybe I would tell her later.

Maybe I'd just let it pass.

If it was meant to be, it would happen.

But me taking a risk out of nowhere wasn't something I usually did.

I had just put my hand on my car door when the house door opened, and Harmony came running out in tight yoga pants and a sports bra, her face flushed.

Everything else faded away.

It was all dewy skin and rosy cheeks and that tight outfit.

So fricking tight.

Just like that, I had no idea what to say, my tongue was tied, and my dick got hard.

Well, hell.

"I'm so sorry, I was in the middle of yoga, trying to work out my lower back, and then I sort of just zoned out and didn't hear the doorbell. It was just luck that I looked out the window and saw your car. I'm sorry." She stopped in front of me, her feet bare even in the cold.

I shook my head, took off my coat, and wrapped it around her.

She looked up at me, her hands brushing the tops of mine as she reached to her own shoulders. A smile played on her lips, and she studied my face.

Was this what the others saw when they said that she looked at me?

I wasn't sure.

I couldn't read her. Maybe it was because I couldn't trust my own feelings when it came to her.

If I could figure her out, maybe I could determine what she would say if I told her how I felt.

What she would say *when* I told her.

"It's too cold for you to be out here in bare feet."

"That is true. Why don't you come in with me? We can talk."

I swallowed hard, looked in her eyes, and tried to see what was there. Tried to imagine what she would say.

I had no idea. I had no idea at all.

And even if I shouldn't want her, I knew I couldn't lie to myself anymore.

I did.

So I took that risk.

"I think we need to talk," I said softly.

Her eyes met mine, curiosity there along with a little something that I couldn't quite name.

"I think we need to talk," I repeated.

And I hoped against all hopes that I didn't ruin what we had.

Anything at all.

CHAPTER THIRTEEN

BRENDON

THROWING up in Harmony's rose bushes sounded like a better idea than anything I could say to her at this moment, but I knew I wouldn't actually do that.

At least, not yet.

She looked up at me, her brows raised as she tightened her grip on the edges of my coat, pulling it closer to her body.

"What's wrong, Brendon?" she asked, her voice low, cautious.

"Let's get inside. You're cold." It took everything within me not to lift her up into my arms, hold her close to my chest, and carry her inside. But she wouldn't want that, at least I didn't think so.

She gave me a weird look, then took my hand in hers, the touch so warm and inviting that I almost jumped. Jesus, I needed to breathe.

"Come on in then. And you can tell me what's going on inside that head of yours."

So, I let her lead me into the house and helped her take off my coat, wondering if I was making a mistake even knowing I needed to make it anyway.

"Okay, why don't you tell me what's on your mind, Brendon? You're kind of scaring me here."

I ran my hand through my hair and started pacing in her entryway, wondering how I was going to start this.

I'd had feelings for her for a while now, and yet for some reason, I hadn't actually thought about what I would say when I told her how I felt.

But it wasn't fair to her for me to have these feelings and hide them from her. Or at least feel like I was hiding. I had tried to walk away, and it hadn't worked. At least, it hadn't yet. Maybe after I told her and she pushed me away, I'd be able to *stay* away. But I wouldn't know until I actually came out with it.

I had to say the words.

"Brendon? Is everything okay with your brothers? Is it the girls? Tell me." She moved to me, stopped me from my pacing, and put her hands on my forearms.

Once again, her touch electrified me, and I looked

down to where her tiny hands were on the corded muscles of my forearms.

She was so small. So fragile.

Breakable in more ways than one.

I couldn't do this. I couldn't break Harmony.

I couldn't bring myself to do it.

Hell.

Stop being a dick. I just needed to do this.

"Brendon," Harmony snapped. "Do you need to go to the hospital? What's wrong?"

"I don't know how to start."

"Then sit down. Or just let it all out. Just tell me."

"Everything's fine. I swear. At least, that I know of. Everything's fine. I do not need to go to the hospital. I might need a drink, but that's beside the point."

She looked at me, studying my face. She didn't let go of my arm.

Maybe that would settle me. Or perhaps it would make it worse. It didn't really matter though, I had to figure this out.

"Okay, everyone's fine. But you clearly aren't. You said we needed to talk. So, what is it?"

"I really don't know where to begin."

"Okay. We can just go sit. Have some coffee. And we can make yours Irish if you really need that drink."

I shook my head and then reached out to her, knowing

I shouldn't, but realizing I was going to do it anyway. I traced my finger along her jawline, and she didn't move back. She didn't startle. She just stood there, studying my face, unmoving.

Then she did move, ever so slightly. She leaned into my touch, and I didn't know if she even knew she had done it. Her pupils dilated, her mouth parted, and I knew I saw desire there. I saw need.

But did she know it was there? Or was it just a reaction?

I was going to make a mistake. But that was fine.

It was my mistake to make.

"Brendon," Harmony whispered. "Tell me."

"I don't know when it began, but it feels like it's been forever—even though I know it hasn't been. Because it wasn't before, it wasn't when it would have been wrong. Though it still feels like it could be wrong."

"You're not making any sense," she said, her voice low. "You're confusing me even more."

"I think *I've* been confused for a lot longer than I care to admit," I said with a rough chuckle that didn't really have any humor in it.

She just looked at me, and I lowered my hand and then traced it down her bare arm, just a touch because I couldn't help myself—or because she didn't pull away. No, she leaned into it.

What was happening? *Is this really happening?*

"I don't know when I started having feelings for you, Harmony, but all I can say is that they're there. And I think of you. I can't stop thinking of you. And I like being near you, I like having you in my life. I like our talks. Our lunches. The fact that we touch each other just because. That we can talk to each other. And I know it's probably wrong, I know I should stop. But I can't. I tried, Harmony. I tried so damn hard. But I can't stay away. And I don't know if I *want* to stay away anymore."

She stood there, and I had no idea what she was feeling, what she was thinking. Had I made a mistake? It felt like I was outside of my body, watching it all happen and trying to deconstruct exactly what was going on. Yet I couldn't. I couldn't figure out what was going on.

I felt like I was losing my mind. Maybe that was right. Perhaps it's what I needed. Harmony didn't say anything, so I continued. "I thought about you. I've always thought about you. No...that's not right."

"You haven't thought about me?" she asked, her voice neutral. Almost too calm.

"I've thought about you since you came back. Since we became friends again. I never thought about you in that way when Moyer was alive. I swear."

I lifted my hands and held my palms out. "You were

always my friend. Even before Moyer, you were my friend. But I've always been drawn to you. To your personality. To your mind. Just to you. And so, in these new circumstances where our strings are tied, irrevocably bound together by our past but not in the same way it used to be, I've thought about you. And I know it's wrong. I've been very careful what I've said to you when we've been near each other recently. And I don't know what to do about it."

She blinked up at me, tilting her head. "You've thought about me?"

I ran my hand through my hair, letting out a ragged breath. "Yes."

"How?"

I didn't even realize I had laughed until the humorless sound came from my body. "Like I want you. Like I want to be near you. Like I want to be beside you. I want you in my life, I just want to spend time with you. And I want to touch you. I want to kiss you. I want to do so much. But those are my desires. It doesn't mean I have to act on any of them. But I can't just stand by and let myself drown in the worry that I'm doing the wrong thing or that I'm not doing enough."

"Does it help that I thought about you, too?" she asked, her voice hesitant, but her eyes resolved, so sure and focused on mine.

I swallowed hard, trying to process exactly what she had just said. "You thought about me, too?"

She let out a small laugh, shaking her head. My heart plummeted.

"You don't think about me?"

She looked up quickly and then reached out to squeeze my free hand. "I've thought about you, Brendon. Believe me. I was just shaking my head because it makes no sense that we're acting this way."

"I've no idea how to act. I feel like I'm having an out-of-body experience at this point."

"I've thought about you. But you've always been my friend, Brendon. It was easier just to be your friend. Because I've always relied on you. And maybe that's why I stepped away when I did because I rely on you too much."

I shook my head, reaching up to cup her face. "You've never leaned on me too much. I give you everything that I have to give, Harmony. You were my friend before, and I would have done that then. But now? With this feeling inside of me? I'd give you anything and more."

"And that scares me. Because the idea that you would do that while not knowing how I feel, even if *I* don't know how I feel, scares me. Because I don't want to bruise you. I don't want to hurt you. You deserve more than that."

"Do I? I think I deserve exactly what I'm getting. Or

maybe what I could get. I don't know, Harmony. But standing here, watching you, not knowing what to do, not knowing if me touching you like this is wrong...it worries me."

"And maybe it should? I don't know. But I like this. And I don't know why I didn't notice it before. I mean, I've always noticed that you've given great hugs. That I can sink into you."

I sighed. "Those hugs killed me sometimes. At least, recently. Because all I want to do is just hug you tighter and smooth your hair and act like some teenage stalker and never let you go."

"That would never be you."

"I thought about it sometimes. Not going to lie."

"We walked away from each other before, at least after Moyer died."

I flinched at my friend's name, even though I had said it before. She just gave me a sad smile. "We walked away from each other because it hurt."

"I was afraid that every time you saw me, you would see him. You would see that I couldn't bring him back. That I hadn't been able to reach out for him in time."

That was part of my pain, the idea that it was my fault that he was dead. She pushed at me but didn't let go. "Seriously? You can never think that. When I look at you, I see Brendon. Maybe I see a different version of you from before, but we all change, right? I saw you as my friend before, I saw you as my husband's friend. And then we stepped away. And maybe we needed to so we could heal. But we're back again. I'm not the same woman I was before."

"And I didn't have these feelings for that woman. I have feelings for the woman that's standing in front of me now."

Harmony blinked away a tear and then let out a curse before using her thumb to wipe away any evidence of it. "Don't cry, Harmony. I can go. Don't cry for me."

"I'm not crying for you. I'm crying for the idea that you see me. You're not seeing the widow. You don't see the friend you had. You're seeing someone different. Someone I'm just starting to get to know. Every time I look at you, I see someone different, too. You've changed, Brendon. Maybe I fought really hard not to see that. I fought so hard to not see the man you've become or the fact that you're not just my friend anymore."

I swallowed hard. "You've seen that man?"

"Maybe I started to really see him when you sat down with me after my first bad date."

I closed my eyes, sighing. "I don't want to think about you dating that guy."

"Well, it lasted for maybe a minute. And I never saw him again. But you were there, right after. You made me smile and think about good things rather than the fact that I suck at dating. Because you need to know that, I'm really terrible at it."

"No, you're not. Those guys are."

"You can say that, but I am the common denominator."

"No, that's those fools."

"You say the nicest things, but I still don't know what I'm doing. I'm learning how to be me now. To be myself as this single person trying to live in the world. And I want companionship, even though I don't know exactly what I want. But you were always there for me. You were there for me right after when I didn't know what I was doing when I felt like I was doing too much. And I was always afraid I would lean on you too much. Rely on you so much that you would break and we would shatter everything that we had."

"And I was afraid that you weren't going to lean on me at all. That somehow you would find someone else to lean on or figure out that you were strong enough and didn't need me. Because I shouldn't want you, Harmony. I shouldn't have you."

"Maybe you should let me decide what I'm allowed to have or not. What I should or shouldn't want or do."

"I've been so careful, Harmony. So careful not to tell you what I'm feeling to the point where I don't know myself. But it was getting so I couldn't actually continue hiding from you like I was. And I didn't like you going out on dates, I didn't like you meeting men who weren't me. And that was selfish."

"Does it help that I got a little jealous of the idea of you dating, too?" Harmony asked and then buried her face in her hands. "And I have no idea why I felt that way. I did so good about thinking of you as my friend. Because you *are* my friend, Brendon. No matter what, I don't want to ruin that. I don't want to change anything there. Though what if it's already changed?"

I didn't know what to say to that, so I just leaned forward and traced my finger over her jawline again. "If you don't want this. You need to tell me."

Her eyes widened, her mouth parted. "Oh. Okay."

She didn't move away, didn't tell me to stop, so I lowered my head and slowly brushed my lips over hers.

It was like coming home. A sweet temptation, a gift. Harmony was soft, willing, and yet...new. This was the person I had hugged so many times in my life but one I would never get the scent of from my mind. I had held her close more times than I could count, and yet this was different. I had kissed her forehead, pecked her cheek, bussed her temple. I'd even kissed her hands.

But I had never kissed her lips.

I hadn't known how soft they were, or that she would taste of mint with a little bit of cucumber water at the end.

I didn't know that she would moan, arch into me as I deepened the kiss.

I had no idea that she would take me to the brink with just a bare touch, make me want to surrender.

I hadn't known that she would bring me to the idea of poetry, the idea of sonnets and words with just the brush of lips.

I wasn't a romantic. I wasn't a poet.

But Harmony led me to that. She was my symphony. My melody. My Harmony.

And it was just a kiss. Our first.

And I hoped to all the gods that it wasn't our last.

When she moaned again just a little, I kissed her harder, but then took a step back, needing to breathe, to just catch my freaking breath.

I leaned my forehead against hers as we both let out ragged breaths, and then I looked into her eyes and laughed.

I shouldn't have laughed. This was romantic, there was nothing funny about it. But then her eyes filled with tears, and she started giggling.

Those weren't sad tears, I knew those kinds of tears.

No, they were ridiculous tears, like the ones I felt pricking at the backs of my eyes.

I didn't cry, not often. It just wasn't what I did. But I knew Harmony's tears.

"Wow," Harmony said, her voice breathy. "Wow."

"I think wow's a good thing to say." I kissed the tip of her nose and then ran my hands through her hair, wondering what to say next. Wondering what to do next. I wasn't good at this. I had never been good at dating, much like Harmony had said about herself. I'd never had a serious girlfriend before. Yes, I was old enough that I probably should have, but it just hadn't happened. And it wasn't like I had been pining for Harmony the whole time.

No, this was relatively new, even though it had settled over a steady relationship I already had with her.

"What does this mean?" she asked me, and I ran my thumb over her cheekbone.

"I think this means I want to do that again."

"Kiss me? Because I could do that."

"That, too. But I want to take you out. For real. Not just lunch between friends. Not where I show up at the end of your date when it's over. I want to take you out. And I want to show you a real date. With me."

"I think I'd like that.

"So, think on it. It's just you and me right now. Only us."

Her smile dimmed slightly, and she shook her head.

"No, it can't ever be. I think you need to understand that. Because, yes, it's you and me, and we're standing right here, and we just kissed and are going on a date. And we're going to figure out exactly what this all means and are going to be very careful with each other. So that part, yes, is you and me. Only you and me. But the rest? It's never only us. It can't be."

My heart didn't hurt at that. Instead, I relaxed as if she had just said the words that gave me permission to actually feel. "I get that. More than I thought possible. It's not only you and me. Because we are what our past made us. So, we're going to make this work. Even with the ghost in the room."

And with that, I kissed her again, just a soft brush of lips. And then I got my coat and walked out the door, leaving her standing there—maybe as irrevocably changed as I was.

Because I had kissed Harmony Wynham, the girl from my past, the woman of my dreams.

Now, of my heart.

I just prayed that we could make this work.

Because the cost of what would happen if it didn't was far too much to bear. For either of us.

CHAPTER FOURTEEN

I said yes. And I know you'd have been happy with that. That's the one thing I do know.
- Harmony to Moyer. 25 months ATE.

HARMONY

I WASN'T GOING to hyperventilate. I was not going to hyperventilate. And if I kept telling myself that, I could maybe, just *maybe*, catch my breath and stop shaking. Because all I could do was focus on breathing in and then breathing out. But I couldn't actually slow down the process.

Instead, the more I thought about breathing, the more I had to suck in that breath and try to actually get oxygen into my lungs. It wasn't easy when all I wanted to do was try not to pass out while thinking about exactly what I was doing.

"You're starting to worry me, honey. What's wrong?" Eleanor asked as she slowly made her way into my office.

I quickly sat up from the desk, clutched at my heart even as I tried to catch my breath, and made my way to her. "What did I say about putting weight on your knee?" I said, helping her into a chair. I'd added more cushions to it so it looked like a plush throne for a queen rather than the guest chair, but the woman refused to stay in her office and off her feet, so I had to do what I had to do.

"I'm fine," she said as she sank into the chair. "You don't look fine. What's wrong?"

I looked down at her, making sure she was indeed okay and not in pain, and then shook my head. "It's work."

"Work? What's wrong? Are you having issues with another account?"

I shook my head quickly, trying to collect my thoughts. "I mean I shouldn't talk about things at work. The account is fine." I'd been able to get a new donation, as well as another facilitator. I didn't have to worry about the son of the man who had cared so much about us ditching us. I didn't have to deal with that any longer. Everything was actually going amazingly well with the foundation and the charity. That meant I knocked on wood often and saved for rainy days, but work was actually going well.

And my personal life might be going better, but I was too stressed out to really think about that.

"Oh, shush. Everyone else is gone for the day, and you're about to head home. Tell me, honey. What's making you so stressed?"

"I'm going on a date with Brendon."

"Oh, really?" Eleanor asked, her eyes dancing as her brows lifted. "It's about time. That young man is so sweet, and you two already spend enough time together. So, tell me, how did it happen? Did he ask you? Did you ask him? Is this your first date with him? Anything has to be better than the last few dates you went on. I mean a rock would be better than the last few dates you've been on."

I leaned against my desk, folded my arms in front of my chest, and shook my head. A smile played on my lips, but I tried not to laugh. I didn't need to encourage the other woman.

"Well?"

"Well? Well, I don't know. I don't know what to say. It seems like it came out of nowhere, but I know that's not the case. I know because I can feel it in here." I put my hand over my heart. "He just came over and told me he'd been thinking about me, that he'd been trying *not* to think about me, and then suddenly he was there, and then his lips were on mine, and then I was saying yes, I did want to go on a date with him. Is this okay? Should I be going out with him? Why am I even asking these questions?"

"That's a lot of questions in a short period of time," Eleanor said, her voice soft as she leaned forward and patted my hand. "I can't answer any of them for you. They're all for you. But I know that boy has always taken care of you. Not as if you couldn't take care of yourself, but in a way that means he's your friend. And I think that's important. You need to be friends with those you're in a relationship with."

She smiled and continued. "You need to have that type of trust. And I know he's been in your life for longer than most of the other people you know, and I'm happy about that. I think you need to live in the moment, even as you get those answers for yourself. But Brendon has always been a good man to you. Always. You should talk it over with your girls. And then you need to smile, put on some lipstick and a wonderful dress, and have fun. Because he puts light in your eyes. Even if you don't notice it."

I swallowed hard. "Really?" I asked. Brendon always made me happy, because he was my friend.

But there was that whole other level to it, the one that I wasn't sure I was prepared for. The things I thought maybe I should deal with anyway.

"He's a wonderful man," Eleanor repeated. "Now, go talk with your friends."

"You *are* my friend, Eleanor."

She laughed. "Oh, I am. But you need to talk to friends your own age. And you need to cry if you need to, laugh if you want to, and just be."

"Just be. That's been my motto for the last couple of years."

"And it's a good one to live by. Now just be, Harmony. And just live."

I hugged her tightly as I leaned forward, then helped her to her driver since she wasn't allowed to drive anymore. Then I made my way home.

I was going on a date tonight. And I was even running a little late because I had spent too much time in my office with Eleanor, trying to figure out exactly what I was feeling. I couldn't really think about what all of that meant if I didn't actually get it out of my system. But I couldn't put any of it into words, so how was I supposed to deal with it?

"I need a drink," I whispered to myself, then went to open a bottle of wine.

Yes, I was going to have a single glass of wine while I got ready for my date, and I needed it. Because there were only so many times in my life—no, that wasn't right. There was only *one* time in my life when I would go on a first date with Brendon Connolly.

I had been to dinner with him, sure. I had been to lunch with him. I had gotten drunk with him and had many nights with him.

But nothing like tonight.

Tonight would be different. The occasion was momentous.

As I looked over at a photo of Moyer and me laughing at the beach, I smiled.

"I'm really doing this," I whispered to the photo, knowing that it was just me, that Moyer wasn't actually around to hear. But I swore I could feel the brush of fingers down my back, and then a gentle hug, telling me it was okay. I didn't cry, because that's not what I felt in the moment. I was Harmony. I was allowed to go on a date. I had been going on dates.

Brendon wouldn't be my first date since Moyer. Though he *had* been my first kiss since Moyer, and I was happy about that.

The fact that he had known Moyer would be tricky, but that was something I was going to deal with. Maybe it would make it easier because Brendon knew that Moyer would always be there. I would never *not* love Moyer. But a heart was a wonderful thing. It allowed you to have a range of emotions, to love more than one person in your life.

Did I love Brendon? Yes, as a friend, and maybe something more. But I needed time, and I needed experience to look deeper into that. To be able to answer that question.

But in order to do that, I actually had to get ready for my date.

I took the first sip from my glass of wine when the doorbell rang.

I looked down at my phone, panicking for a moment, and then remembered that thanks to Eleanor, my girls were on their way to my house so I didn't have to be alone before my first date.

Not my first date ever, but my real first date with Brendon.

There went that hyperventilating thing again.

I set down my wine glass and made my way to the front door, hoping I'd actually be able to keep my breathing together.

"Okay, let's see what we can do," Violet said as she pushed past me, Sienna on her heels. I just looked at them.

"What do you mean, what you can do? Is there something wrong with me?"

Sienna just laughed, and Violet shook her head. "There's nothing wrong with you. But you need to breathe. Because I know you're not breathing. You're blushing, your cheeks are bright red, and your eyes have this manic, wide thing going on. So, just breathe. We're here for you."

"Oh, great. You can see that I'm freaking out? What's Brendon going to think?" Why couldn't I do this right? I liked him. I loved him. He was my friend. Yes, things were different. They had been for a while now. What was I going to do?

"Brendon's going to think you're amazing. That you're so amazing, he probably should've asked you out before you went out with those other guys. But he didn't, so now you have funny stories to talk about. But let's just get you into something cute, and let you finish that glass of wine I see on the counter over there. Everything's going to be wonderful."

"You're making me panic again. Why can't I just wear what I'm already wearing?" I asked looking down at my pencil skirt and blouse. "I think it looks just fine."

"You look gorgeous. Fucking gorgeous. But you're not ready for a date." Sienna put her hands on her hips, pushing her shoulder bag out of the way. "Now, don't worry. We'll get you ready."

"You're starting to really stress me out."

"You were stressed out before we even got here," Violet said as she walked over to the kitchen. Her heels click-clacked across my hardwood floor, and I swore my heartbeat matched the rhythm.

Click. Clack. Click. Clack.

Beat.

Deep breath.

Beat.

Deep breath.

Beat.

Deep breath.

I couldn't actually focus. Why had I said I would go out with him? Just because I'd started to think about him differently and always wanted to talk to him didn't mean that I should go on a date with him.

"Well, you are," Sienna said.

My head shot up, and I looked between them as Violet handed me my glass of wine. "Did I actually say that out loud?"

"Yes, you did. Now, why don't you word-vomit everything else on your mind so you get it out of your system before you go on this date with Brendon?"

"I'm going on a date with your boyfriend's brother." I let out a groan and took a big gulp of wine. "Your boyfriend's brother."

"That's just one of his many labels," Violet said before taking my wine glass away. "That's enough wine for you."

I pouted. "That was just one sip."

"No, that was like a big gulp. Like half the glass. You don't need to be drunk to go on a date with Brendon. You go out to eat with him all the time. You have drinks with him all the time. He owns a bar with his brothers."

"But this is different."

"Of course, it's different. But it's fine. Everything's going to be fine."

I looked at Violet as she said the words and just shook my head.

"I think I'm more stressed out now than I was before."

"That's fine. Get it all out now. That's what we're here for."

"To stress me out?"

"Well, we're here for many things."

"To annoy me?" I asked.

"Now you're just being rude," Sienna said, shaking her head even though she smiled.

"I know I'm not making any sense, and I know I'm being rude. Why did I say I would do this?"

Violet reached out and gripped my shoulders. "Because you want to. You are so strong, Harmony. So damn strong."

I swallowed hard, used to that phrase. Everyone called

223

me strong. It was hard not to appear that way when you actually survived one of the worst things a person could live through.

When you felt as if you were dying inside, it was hard to appear anything *but* strong to others when trying to find your new normal.

I had lived my life. I had found my way out of the ashes. I had survived. I had lost my future, my happiness, my husband. But I had fought my way through it, even through the haze, even through the numbness.

I had done all of that, so people called me strong.

Though most days I didn't believe it. Most days, it was just a hashtag that didn't make any sense.

But when my friends said it to me, I tried to believe it. Because they weren't saying it to be mean. They weren't saying it when there wasn't anything else to say. They said it because they believed it to be true. Because they knew I needed to hear it. Even if it wasn't easy.

"I just don't want to mess things up."

"It's heavy. Life is heavy. But you can do this."

I leaned into Violet, giving her a hug. Sienna wrapped her arms around us, and I sniffed a bit. I wasn't crying. Not yet. That might come later, though. I couldn't help it.

"I don't even know what to wear."

"We're going to help you with that. We're going to

help you with everything. It's going to be like a *Pretty Woman* moment.

"But I'm not a hooker. And I do kiss on the lips."

That sent them into peals of laughter, and I just shook my head.

"Allison would be better at this. She was always good at figuring out the best outfits for different kinds of dates."

I looked at my friends as I said our other friend's name. There were no tears this time because we were all being as strong as we could be. And there was that word again. *Strong*. We were getting used to it.

"Well, she did have better taste than all of us."

"Hey," Sienna said as she looked over at her sister. "I have just fine taste."

"Yes, you do, but Allison was still better at figuring out exactly what outfit made us feel better," Violet said. "Now, what would Allison do?"

I pushed back the sadness I felt because, yes, it was hard, but we had to be strong and think and talk about Allison so she wouldn't be forgotten.

But tonight wasn't about that. Tonight was about my first date with Brendon.

"Okay, I'm going out with a man that I've known since he was a boy. Since I was a girl. A man I knew before Moyer. One that was my friend, and then Moyer's friend. And then, somehow, we were all friends, and I was married to Moyer. Brendon was also there when my husband died. He's the man who held me when I cried."

"You sound like a country song now," Violet put in, wincing. "Sorry."

"I didn't mean to rhyme," I said, pinching the bridge of my nose.

"But you do it all the time," Sienna said, laughing.

"Stop it. I'm trying to get through my feelings here, and you're trying to make me laugh." I shook my head at the two of them, but they just smiled at me.

"Continue on," Violet said a bit pompously.

"Okay. Where was I?"

"Rhyming?" Sienna said.

This was like the worst time to be laughing like this, when I was talking about such deep and serious topics. But this was us. It was how we got through things, being the lovable dorks we were. "Okay. And then we—Brendon and me—weren't that close anymore, not for a while. But then Cameron came back, and we didn't want to lose the bar, so we all became friends again. And then I got closer to Brendon, and somehow he asked me out. Everything's going to be okay. It's just...it's a lot."

"I know it's a lot," Violet said. "But we're real people with real emotions. And we have paths that happen to be very complicated with lots of tangles. But I see the way he looks at you, and I see the way you look at him."

I swallowed hard. "Really?"

"Yes. Of course."

"But like...not before, right? Because he said it wasn't before. When it would've been wrong."

"No, it wasn't before. It's this now thing. We've all said that we aren't the same people we were before, and that's important."

"Okay. But what am I doing?" I asked and then promptly burst into tears.

I didn't mean to. I didn't cry often. But the tears just kept coming. Suddenly, Violet was holding me, and Sienna was trying to dab my face with tissues even though I pushed her away.

"What am I doing? I know this isn't my first date, but this is like a *real* first date," I repeated, even though they hadn't been here when I said that before. "The others were all practice dates. But this is real. This means something. This is Brendon. Brendon fucking Connolly. If I go on a date with him, and something actually happens, could this be a future? Or what if everything gets messed up and we break up and then we can't even hang out at the bar anymore? I can't hang out with you? What if it all gets broken? What if I break everything because I fall in love with him? What if I'm already in love with him? There's something inside me that I know is there. Every time I look at him, I feel something, and I can't breathe."

I tried to take a deep breath, but I couldn't, my lungs were constricting. "This is real."

Sienna just looked at me, dug around in her purse, and then handed me a paper bag.

A fricking paper bag.

"Where did you get this?" I screeched, my lungs burning.

"Well, I have them for emergencies like this." Sienna just looked at me and blinked. I blinked back.

"Like this? Really? Like how I'm freaking out over my dead husband and his friend and the fact that I'm going out on a real date? And you just have this paper bag for this exact emergency?" I asked. I knew I sounded ridiculous, but this seemed like a very absurd situation.

"Well, it's not like I labeled the damn thing. Are you okay? Do you actually need the bag? I really just had it in my purse earlier for my lunch and then kept it so I didn't waste it, but you know...whatever."

I looked at the paper bag and just started laughing. "I'm losing my mind."

"No, you're not losing your mind," Violet said, rubbing my shoulders. "You just needed to get that all out of your system."

"I love Moyer. Not just loved, I *love* him. But I know he's not coming back. And I know that I'm allowed to fall in love with someone else and go on other dates. I went on that first blind date not feeling this emotion that I do now. What's wrong with me?" I asked.

"The others didn't matter. You said they were practice. And they were. This matters. And it's really okay that it matters."

I looked between my friends and then looked down at that paper bag. I started laughing. "You are a riot, Sienna."

"I know. But that's why you love me."

And so, I leaned on my friends, hugged them both tightly, and then we found the perfect dress for me to wear. Because I was going on a date with Brendon Connolly. The man from my past. From my present. And in some way, a part of my future.

Tonight, I would be one step closer to figuring out what that future was.

It was okay that I was conflicted. Being stressed out was okay.

Apparently, I just needed a paper bag to figure that out.

CHAPTER FIFTEEN

BRENDON

WHEN HARMONY OPENED THE DOOR, I think I swallowed my tongue.

I knew that was just an expression, but as I tried to open my mouth to speak, I actually choked a bit.

"Wow," I said and then shook my head. I cleared my throat and tried to actually articulate what I was thinking. What I was feeling. Instead, all that came out again was, "Wow."

"Well, I think that reaction is exactly what I needed," Harmony said with a laugh and then shook her head. Her long, auburn curls fell over her shoulders in soft waves, and it took everything within me not to reach out and just tug on a couple of the tendrils, to feel that silky hair along my skin.

She had done up her eyes in this smoky makeup that accentuated her beauty.

I had seen her with makeup and without it, and I loved her both ways. I just liked whatever made her happy.

And, yeah, I was a sap, but I couldn't really help it. I was going on a date with Harmony. And I hadn't thrown up yet. I counted that as a win.

She had on a champagne-colored top and charcoal pants that hugged her butt. I couldn't actually see her butt, but I could see the fact that they hugged her hips and so I inferred. I noticed the tips of her high heels peeking out from under her pant legs and swallowed hard again as my gaze traveled up, past her curves to those eyes of hers. The ones that saw too much, that I couldn't stop looking at.

"I had on a dress, and then thought it was too cold. And then I realized I didn't know where we were going, so I went with pants. But I can change again. If you want."

She bit her lip, and I swallowed hard.

"I want to take you to that Brazilian steakhouse that we talked about. So, what you're wearing's fine. You can wear jeans or a burlap bag for all I care. You look fucking amazing."

I let out a rough chuckle and shook my head. "I'm usually better at words than this, but you kind of blew me away."

I couldn't really focus, not when she looked at me like that, but I was going to do my best.

"Well, you don't look too bad yourself," she said, smiling at me. "And I love Brazilian steakhouses, so that sounds great."

I reached out and took her hand, pulling her towards me. And because I knew that this was a first—a first of many firsts—I went slow. I waited for her to look up at me and for her lips to part ever so slightly before I pressed my lips to hers.

I kissed her softly, just a taste, just a beginning. An appetizer.

And then I smiled against her lips.

"I wanted to do that before I was too nervous to do it later."

"There's nothing about you that's nervous, Brendon. You're one of the most confident guys I know."

"It's all a façade."

"Not completely. Oh, I'm glad you think that. Because I'm pretty sure I would have been nervous throughout the whole evening thinking about it."

I helped her close the door and lock it, and then we made our way to my car, both of us acting a little nervous as if we weren't quite sure what to do with each other. We had eaten out together countless times. Even in romantic settings. But it had never been like this. Yes, I had been nervous around her because I was doing my best not to think about her the way I always was. I was trying to make things seem normal. Now, things weren't really normal anymore at all. They were different.

I'd put in a reservation at one of my favorite places, and they sat us quickly. It was one of those steakhouses where you go up for the salad bar area and eat as much as you want, though most people didn't eat that much at all. After all, you didn't want to load up on carbs and salad and all the amazing soups and bread and not have room for meat that we were about to be offered.

This particular steakhouse also had the side-dishes at the buffet area, rather than bringing potatoes and mushrooms and vegetables directly to the table for the party to share. So we could take exactly what we wanted, and then come back to have our wine, and then eat meat.

A lot of meat.

Men in oddly tight pants and knee boots with puffy shirts came around the room, each holding a different big fork or what looked like a large blade. They held the end of the short sword in one hand and the dish to catch all of the trimmings in the other. They went from each table and offered up their meat. It was just about every type of meat. Braised pork tenderloin, chicken, about eighteen kinds of beef all cooked different ways and marinated differently. There was lamb, and even bacon-wrapped things. My mouth watered just thinking about it all. As long as you had your little coasters set to green, they would come to your table and slice off pieces to your specifications right on your plate. They even gave you little tongs so you could help them and it didn't splatter everywhere.

I loved the place. It was a little fun, and we could eat as much as we wanted. Harmony always ate as much as she wanted in front of me, she wasn't like some of my dates where they only ate salad because they were either really in love with greens or afraid I would judge them. I was of the mind that you should eat whatever you wanted. Have fun with food.

But not everyone thought that.

"Aiden would probably hate this place," I said as we sat down, looking around.

Harmony just laughed. "Well, you know him, he's very particular about place settings and presentation. But he might have fun. He could try a bunch of things without having to be stuck with just one thing or two."

"You can never go out with Aiden to certain places. He will order like eight different plates so we can all share them and he can taste everything. And then we bring it home and end up eating it for the next couple of days."

"That actually sounds amazing," Harmony said, laughing. "I mean, sometimes, I can't make a decision and want to try everything. Or, there are some places that I go where I love this one meal and get it every time and never get to try anything else because I'm afraid."

"You are not really going to have that problem here. You can literally taste every single thing. But there are some things that you don't want to eat too much of because then you won't have enough room for meat."

Our gazes met, and then we each threw our heads back and laughed. The tension slid out of us, and any nervousness was suddenly gone. We were just Brendon and Harmony. It might not last for too long, but for that exact moment? I loved it.

"Oh God, I wonder how many penis jokes they have to deal with. I mean, they're men in really tight pants, coming around showing off swords and meat and meeting your eyes as they slowly slice and give you a little bit of their meat."

I closed my eyes and groaned. "Maybe this wasn't the best place to take you?"

"No, I love this place. I haven't actually been to this one, though. I went to one just like it, just a different franchise. Moyer used to love it, so we went there a few times. I think that was in downtown Colorado Springs."

Harmony met my gaze, her face paling. "Crap. I'm sorry. I'm really not good at dating. I told you that. I shouldn't just bring up Moyer like that."

"Harmony." I whispered the word, putting my hand out so I could trace my fingers along her elbow. "It's okay. You were right before. He's always here. And you are going to talk about him. I'm going to talk about him. Hell, he was a huge part of my life, too. I know this is weird, and we're going to have to figure out exactly what we are to each other, but we are allowed to bring him up. I think it will make it more awkward and worse for both of us if we *don't* bring him up."

"I know. And the fact that you get that means everything to me. And, let me just say, that before you got to my house when the girls were helping me pick out something to wear, I was really afraid I wouldn't be able to eat. That I would be too nervous and not be able to swallow anything. I was so stressed out. But not only is this place fricking amazing, and I'm going to stuff my face, *you* are amazing. And you always put me at ease, even if I know I'm probably going to say something stupid."

"Well, I'm probably going to be the one putting my foot in my mouth first. So, are we ready for the salad bar? Or meat?"

She flashed me a grin and then flipped her coaster over to green. Apparently, we were going for meat.

I was stuffed by the time we got through seven different types of red meat, three different kinds of pork, and three different types of chicken. I didn't even know that there were that many parts of a cow, but I was learning.

"I'm still hungry," Harmony said, groaning. "I'm really glad I wore these pants and not the other ones, because these give me a little room." Harmony laughed as she said the words, and I snorted.

"You know, if I went on a date with anyone else, they probably wouldn't mention things like that."

When her eyes narrowed, I quickly held out my hands. "All I'm saying is I'm comfortable. You're comfortable. And it makes me happy. And know that I'm also wearing my pants with give because I'll probably have to roll myself out of here."

"And you know we haven't even gotten to the best part yet," Harmony said, her voice a little sultry.

I swore my dick heard her words and hardened just a bit, even though I felt nothing close to being even remotely sexy at that point.

"Oh?" I asked, my voice a deep growl.

"Yes, there's the pineapple. You know the pineapple? The one they roast over that open fire next to all the meat and then put that brown sugar glaze over it? And then they come out and cut you a slice right off the skewer?" Her head rolled back, and she looked at the ceiling. "It's literally orgasmic."

I got hard, my dick at full attention. It didn't matter that this was our first time out together like this, that we were friends going on a date in the middle of a very complicated situation. She'd just said the word *orgasmic*, and I had no more brain cells left to actually formulate a thought.

"Pineapple. I don't think I've ever actually had the pineapple here. It seemed a waste to fill myself with fruit when I could have more steak."

"Now you're just being blasphemous," Harmony said, reaching out and trailing her fingers along mine. I flipped my hand so I could grab hers, giving it a squeeze. And then I didn't let go.

I watched the breath catch in her throat, and her eyes dilated a bit.

She was beautiful. Stunning. And she was on a date with me. It was just the two of us—at least in the flesh.

I knew I would never actually be any of her firsts. Technically, she wasn't going to be any of mine either. Moyer would always be between us. Always. He would always be around. I would always be second in some cases.

But maybe that was okay. Perhaps it was fine to not be first all the time. It was okay for me to be exactly who Harmony needed me to be. Or maybe I was saying it all wrong in my head. I was really glad I wasn't saying it aloud.

She must have seen something cross my face because she frowned, giving my hand a squeeze.

"What is it? We don't have to have pineapple."

"Oh, we're getting you some pineapple. I was just thinking. I'm really glad you said yes. And I'm glad I actually found the nerve to ask you on a date."

She gave me a small smile, her hand still in mine. "I'm really glad you asked, too. Because I couldn't stop thinking about you before, and I love the fact that we're always together. It's like there was this step I didn't know I needed to take, that kept pushing me towards these dates as I tried to figure out what I was missing. And then you were there. All along, you were there. I was just too blind to see."

I wanted to reach across the table and hold her close, but we couldn't do that. I couldn't touch her the way I wanted. Not now.

"Well, we're here now. And I'm going to get you some of that pineapple."

She just shook her head, smiling. "You need to have some, too. To truly understand what I mean."

"Well, you're saying it's orgasmic. I guess I need to know."

I watched her throat work as she swallowed hard, and I figured we should probably stop talking about orgasms on our first date. Because I didn't think she was ready for that.

Of course, now that I was thinking about it, I couldn't actually breathe. So, when the man came around with the pineapple on a sword, I almost missed him. But he sliced us each off a piece. I thanked him, and we each turned our coasters to red. There would be no more meat for either of us.

And, yes, I did hold back voicing a joke about that. Mostly because there were only so many dick jokes you could make when your own was hard.

"Okay, take a bite," Harmony said, holding out her fork to me.

"I thought you wanted your precious pineapple. You're not going to waste it on me, are you?"

"Of course, I'm not going to waste it on you. I'm just going to take a bite of yours later. But you have to take a bite. Come on. Just one bite."

"Said Eve to Adam," I whispered.

"You know she gets a bad rap for that."

"Oh, I know. And we don't have to get into it. But, I will take a bite." My lips wrapped around the fork. As I pulled back, taking my first taste of that pineapple, I was about to try and speak with my mouth full and make a joke, but I was too busy moaning.

Dear, God. Pineapple. I never knew it could be this good. I never knew that sugar-covered, fire-roasted pineapple could be the glory of the gods. Was this ambrosia? Was I now an immortal?

All these ridiculous thoughts went through my head, but I just stared at Harmony, who looked like the cat who'd gotten the cream, taking her first bite of pineapple as she looked at me.

"I was right, wasn't I?" she asked, looking very right-eous and *very* sexy.

"Oh, you were right. I'm not sure why we didn't just order the entire pineapple for ourselves."

"Because, Mr. Connolly, too much of a good thing will make your teeth rot."

"Is that really the saying?"

"No, it's mostly what I'm telling myself so I don't tackle that man with the sword and eat the entire pineapple. It's why I get it at the end, so I just have a tiny bit of room left in my stomach. But, it's like the best thing ever, isn't it?"

"I think I'm still drooling," I said, and we finished our pineapple, laughing.

By the time we got near her place, we were both

laughing and groaning just a little bit about how full we were, but we were no longer uncomfortably full. It was chilly out, so we hadn't walked anywhere after our meal to work it off, but that was fine. I just wanted to be near her. I didn't want the date to end.

So, when we pulled into her driveway, and I helped her out of the car and led her to the front door, I walked as slowly as I could. I really didn't want to say goodbye. I was afraid that this might be the last time. That while we hadn't made a mistake, it might be the only time.

Maybe we would go back to the way things were because she had gotten it out of her system. But I would never get this out of my system.

I was in love with Harmony.

And I had no idea what to do about it.

We stood at her door, and she looked up at me, her eyes wide, and her mouth parted. "Kiss me?" she asked, her voice soft.

I cupped her face and lowered my head to hers. "You never have to ask that." Before she could say anything else, I kissed her softly, treating her like the treasure she was, like the woman she was.

Her arms wrapped around me, and I moaned, wanting her taste, needing her. She tasted of that pineapple, of our dinner, and just Harmony.

She was everything I had ever wanted.

And when she pulled away, my breath came out in rapid pants. So did hers.

We stood on her porch where anyone could see us, and it was like I was standing at the edge of what my future could be, afraid if I looked too closely, I would see my past again and run. Or she would see it and not take that next step.

So, when she looked at me, her eyes dark and full of promise, I was afraid of what she was going to say.

"Come in with me?" she asked. I froze.

"Are you sure? I mean, I can go, give you some time to yourself."

"Brendon, I know you. You know me. And I know what I want. If it's too soon, you can walk away. But I've looked at you all night, and I've thought about you, and I know what I want. I know it might be rushing things for other people, but it's you and me. It's always been you and me. So I'd love for you to come in with me, and for you to hold me. And for us to see what happens next. Because I feel like I've been waiting a lifetime for this, and now you're here. I don't want to stop. I don't want this night to end."

I didn't know what to say to that. I felt as if Harmony had bared her soul to me. I was broken, fractured pieces of the man I had been before I met Harmony.

So, I didn't say anything at all. Instead, I kissed her hard again, needing her taste, craving her.

And then I followed her in.

And I knew...I knew it wasn't a mistake. I just hoped I would still think that in the morning.

CHAPTER SIXTEEN

You're my favorite Connolly.

- Harmony in a text to Brendon

HARMONY

I WASN'T SCARED. Should I have been? No, I didn't think I could be scared with Brendon.

His lips were on mine, his fingers trailing down my arms, and all I could do was close my eyes and live in the moment.

I knew this was fast, that everything was too fast, yet I

felt as if I had been living in slow motion for the months he had been back. For the time that he had been back in my life and we were friends, though not more than friends.

We had inside jokes, we had smiles for only each other. We even had a dance that was just ours. One that no one else knew.

We had won a pool league together, and we were each other's.

He knew my secrets—at least some of them. And I knew some of his. Not all of them, but not all of them were mine to know.

If I thought about it too hard, I would stop thinking entirely and would likely run away and not want to do anything. I would stop living in the moment, and I would stop wanting Brendon's lips on mine, his hands on me.

But I didn't want to stop thinking.

I wanted to live in the now.

Because this felt right.

All of those other dates had been practice—not even true dates. Because Brendon had always been there.

With him, I wasn't a widow. I wasn't a wife. I wasn't a label.

I was Harmony-fucking-Wynham, and I wanted Brendon Connolly. I wanted this moment.

I had wanted it for longer than I cared to admit. Just

because it had taken me so long to realize what Brendon was to me, who he *could be* to me, didn't mean that I hadn't thought about it. That I hadn't noticed him. The way he filled out a pair of jeans. I'd always appreciated his forearms, his smile, his eyes.

I noticed the way he made me feel, even if I didn't want to feel it.

Some part of me had shielded myself from that, maybe because I was scared.

But I wasn't scared anymore. Not like that.

So, when he kissed me, I leaned into it and wanted more.

"I want to take you to bed, Harmony, in a house that's yours. I want to make love to you, and I want to kiss you, and I want to touch you. Will you let me do that? Or should I walk away?"

"Are those my only options?" I asked in a breathy voice. I sounded like a seductress, something I hadn't felt in far too long.

Brendon made me feel sexy. He made me feel like a woman. And though I could feel like that on my own, Brendon did it with just one look.

That was how I knew this was right. Because he was asking. Because of how he made me feel.

And because I burned for him. I wanted him.

I wasn't walking away.

Not now.

Not tonight.

And maybe not ever again. But that was for another day.

"You can have whatever you want from me, Harmony. That was always the case."

"I want to touch you. I want you to touch me. But if it's too much, I want you to know that it's not you."

He just shook his head, his eyes dancing with humor, warmth...love? No, maybe not that. But there was *something* there. An emotion I couldn't name, something that meant he cared. Said that he was mine. And not only for tonight. Because that wasn't Brendon. He wouldn't cross this line and change who we were to each other if it was just for one night.

And, yes, I was probably taking too many steps without looking back, but this was Brendon.

And we were different.

Anyone who didn't understand that didn't know us.

"Take me to bed," I whispered, and then he bent down, put his arms under my legs, and lifted me to his chest.

I let out a shocked gasp and wrapped my arms around his neck.

"Wow," I whispered. "I knew you were strong. I mean, I have seen you work out, but wow."

He grinned and kissed the tip of my nose. "Well, I am trying to look very manly for you."

I just laughed. "You don't have to try too hard, Brendon."

"I never feel like I have to try around you. Even if I tried not to act that way before."

"We can talk about the whys later, we can talk about everything. Tomorrow. For now, it's just us. And I know it's fast, but I can't stop wanting you."

"And that's okay with me. Because I've always wanted you, Harmony. Simply for us."

And then his mouth was on mine, and we were in my bedroom.

There were no more words then. At least I didn't think there would be. There didn't need to be.

He knew what this was, and so did I.

This would be my first time with anyone since I lost Moyer. But he wasn't in my mind just then, not really. He wasn't in the room. He never had been.

This was my house, my life. And this was my present. And maybe my future.

This was about Brendon and me.

This was a new beginning, and I was going to live in the moment.

Brendon slowly unzipped my jacket, and it fell to the floor, and then he undid his, as well.

We both kicked them out of the way, and then he kissed down my neck and up to my jaw. He bit slightly, and I moaned. Then his lips were on mine again, nibbling, licking, sucking.

My hands tugged at the bottom of his shirt, pulling it out of his pants, and then I slid my hands up his warm back, scraping my nails down his skin.

He let out a groan, and I moaned again.

I could hardly think, I could barely breathe, but he was so sweet, so tender, so Brendon.

This was just like him.

Everything he did was in an effort to care for others, to think about them.

He worshipped me like I was the only thing in his universe.

And that was how I knew this was perfect.

It was how I knew it always had to be Brendon.

"It's you," I whispered. "It's always been you."

"Same here. It's always been you, Harmony."

And then he kissed me again, and my hands moved to his front to undo his shirt's buttons.

He pulled back when I had trouble with one of the top ones, but then he was shirtless, wearing only his pants and shoes and belt. I stood there, my eyes raking down the length of him.

He was so toned, so muscled.

250

He wore suits well, as if he had been born in them. Though I knew that was the exact opposite. I knew all about his past, all about what had been done to him. I could even see some of the scars from that, but then I saw the strength in him, how much he put into his body and his soul.

That was who he was with me.

And that's exactly why this was what I needed.

Why he was the exact perfect person for me.

I leaned forward, kissed his chest, licked gently, and then bit down. His hands roamed all over my body, and I did the same to him. And when he pulled off my shirt, I let my head fall back, and he worshipped me.

He cupped my breasts, molding them in my lace bra, and then he undid the clasp in the front and slowly pulled the straps from my shoulders.

My breasts felt heavy, my nipples hard, aching.

He lowered his head and sucked one into his mouth, gently, oh so gently.

Everything about Brendon was gentle.

He was so huge, so much larger than me. His hands were big, everything about him was big. But he was gentle.

And when he finished with one breast, he moved on to the other, slowly worshipping me like I was a goddess.

I'd never thought I would be able to feel like this

again, feel it all, but Brendon pushed all thoughts from my mind, so I was just there. With him.

In the moment.

And when my knees went weak, he picked me up again and laid me in the middle of the bed.

He slowly took off my shoes and then undid my pants. I wiggled free of them, and then he took my panties down with them.

Suddenly I was bare before him, him in only his boxer briefs, and me naked, wanting.

I hadn't even known he had taken off his pants, and I was sad to have missed it.

Maybe he would let me see it again. Maybe I'd be able to strip them from him myself.

I wanted that.

I wanted more than tonight. I wouldn't have risked everything for just one night.

And I knew Brendon was the same.

He hovered over me then, kissing me softly, and I moaned.

Everything was sweet, innocent. It was as if it was our first time, our first everything.

He slowly kissed down my shoulders, gently touching me, wanting me.

I pressed my thighs together, needing sensation. I was

on the edge of...*something*, but he just kept touching me, making me feel as if I were the only person in the world.

The only person in *his* world.

And when he kissed between the valley of my breasts, I arched for him, wanting more.

My hand slid into his hair, tugging slightly, and he just groaned, licking and biting down my stomach.

And then his head was between my legs, kissing me, sucking, licking.

I had one leg over his shoulder, the other pinned down as he slowly brought me to ecstasy.

I came, my back arched, his name a breath on my lips.

Just a whisper because I had nothing left to say. All I knew was that this man was perfect for this moment.

He was perfect for me.

I was blessed. And I was happy.

And then he was over me, kissing me again.

I didn't know where he had gotten a condom, but I was lucky that he had thought of it.

Because I couldn't think of anything but wanting him inside me.

He sheathed himself, and then he hovered over me, his weight on his hands, his eyes full of concern even as I knew he was shaking with need.

I was shaking, too.

"I can stop anytime you want me to, Harmony. Will you let me inside?"

"It's you," I repeated. "It's always been you."

And so I nodded and let my legs fall to the sides.

And then he was in me, inch by agonizingly slow inch, and his gaze never left mine.

He leaned over me, his weight now on his forearms as our fingers tangled together.

We held hands as he slid in to the hilt.

As our breaths caught, and our eyes remained connected, he moved.

Simple thrusts, soft and achingly slow. And I moved with him.

I could hardly breathe, could barely blink.

I could just watch him and know that this was exactly the perfect moment, the one I needed. The perfect moment *we* needed.

This was making love. It was the next phase of that new normal.

This was just me and Brendon.

He was so soft, so sweet. And yet hard. And I knew there was an edge to him that he held back. That was something I wanted to see.

But not now.

Now, this was exactly what we both needed.

When he let go of one of my hands to slide it between us, I came, needing him, wanting him.

He came then as well, his lips on mine but our eyes still open.

This was Brendon.

My Brendon.

This is what I had truly needed but didn't know.

He was my first.

He was my everything.

And as he held me, the tears fell, but I wasn't sad.

I was happy.

This was that pure bliss, that ultimate happiness that I hadn't known I could feel again.

He held me, and I cried.

And I was happy.

So happy.

CHAPTER SEVENTEEN

BRENDON

SHE HAD CRIED.

Harmony had cried after we made love.

And though she smiled, even though I saw happiness in those tears, I felt like something was breaking inside of me. Scratching to come out as I held it down, wanting to find that breath even though I couldn't.

Harmony had cried, and it was all my fault.

I shouldn't have done this. We had moved too quickly, and I was already screwing everything up.

We should have gone on more dates than just our first before I went to bed with her. Hell, maybe I should have just remained her friend before I stirred everything up.

But there was no going back.

Harmony and I had had sex, the best sex of my life—soft, sweet, and so fucking perfect.

And then she had cried.

I hadn't left right after that. No, I stayed.

I'd held her through the night, and though her tears had quickly dried, I didn't leave.

We didn't make love again. Instead, we stayed up until the sun had almost begun to rise and just talked.

We talked about nothing and everything, and it felt like we were back to normal. Except for the whole fact that we were both still naked, still covered in each other's scents, and touching each other—slow caresses as if neither of us realized we were doing it.

But we were still touching each other. Still acting as if she hadn't cried.

Women cried after sex. Men cried after sex.

Their first time together?

I just didn't know what to think. I felt like I was making mistake after mistake. Yes, this was my fucking dream come true. I loved this woman.

But I didn't like seeing her in pain.

So, I didn't know what to do next. Oh my God, I didn't want to let Harmony go. Because if I did, the dream would end, the bubble would burst, and I'd have to face the morning.

I somehow fell asleep with her in my arms, softly curled into me as we slept for a few hours.

And when her alarm went off the next morning, we both groaned.

"Why does morning have to come so early?" she asked, laughing. I opened one eyelid, and she covered her face. "Don't look at me. And don't smell my breath. I need a shower and to brush my teeth. And coffee. Oh, and to look human before you look at me. I mean, the morning after is supposed to be pretty. I'm not supposed to look like this. You're not supposed to see me like this."

And even though my emotions and thoughts were in a whirlwind, I couldn't help but laugh. "Oh, shut up." And then I kissed her hard, hovering over her as I covered her body with mine. "You look amazing. Beautiful. Perfect." I kissed her nose.

She rolled her eyes and pushed at my chest. "Oh, shut up. I have bed-head, sex hair, and who knows what my breath smells like. We didn't actually brush our teeth before we went to sleep. So now I have like sex, pineapple, meat breath." Her whole body blushed as she closed her eyes and giggled. "Well, not exactly your meat breath since we didn't get to that point."

I burst out laughing, my whole body shaking. "Oh, God, I'm never going to be able to think about blowjobs the same way again. Meat breath?"

"That's such a Sienna thing to say."

I let out a groan. "Don't say Sienna when I'm naked and hovering over you, and my very hard cock is sitting right between your thighs."

"Well, I did notice that, but I wasn't going to say anything." She winked, and I laughed again.

"But, really, don't mention the girls. They're like my sisters."

"And I'm not?"

I shook my head, laughing again. "Well, if you're my sister, then what we did last night would probably be illegal in a few states. Or all of them. I actually don't know anymore, but we're just going to say it'd be wrong."

"Well, I'm not your sister. And the girls technically aren't either."

"But I feel like they are. And one of them is marrying Cameron, so she actually will be my sister."

"He hasn't asked her yet," Harmony whispered.

"But he will. Any day now."

Harmony's eyes widened. "Do you know something I don't?"

I shook my head. "No, but it's just written in the stars. When he's ready, when she's ready, he'll ask. But it's sort of a foregone conclusion."

"You know, I don't actually believe in those, mostly because I need to see it in writing first, or just because nothing's actually foregone, but with those two...I believe it."

I played with a strand of her hair, something I'd wanted to do all night and was apparently still doing. "They're perfect for each other. Right for each other."

"I'm just sad that it took so long for them to get there. You know?"

I leaned over to the side so I wasn't squishing her anymore, but we were still pressed tightly together. "Sometimes, you just have to wait for the right moment. Wait for enough time to pass so you're the right person at that exact moment."

I knew I wasn't talking about Cameron and Violet any longer. Not exactly. But then again, I wasn't being very subtle about it.

"Exactly."

I looked down at her and knew I loved her. But then I remembered those tears.

I didn't know what to make of them, and I felt like we both needed a moment to breathe, a beat to think before I said something stupid like that I loved her.

"I need to go home and shower and get ready for work."

"It's Saturday."

"But I work two jobs now, and bars are kind of busy on Saturdays."

"Would it be weird if I came by later? To see you, but the bar, too. I haven't been by in too long. I've been a little busy with everything."

"I don't want it to be weird. I want to see you again. I want to see you as my friend. I want you to be at the bar. And I want to see you as my..." I trailed off.

"Yeah, we should probably talk about that label thing. I hate labels."

"I know what you mean. But I'll see you later today? At the bar?"

"Of course." She reached up and grabbed my face, and I leaned down to take her lips.

The kiss deepened, and I groaned, pulling back as her alarm went off again.

"Why is your alarm going off on a Saturday?"

"Because I have to work out and then deal with all my household things before I can actually enjoy my weekend. But you should head home so you can make it to work on time. But, Brendon? I had a wonderful time. And...just thank you. I know it's weird to say thank you, but I don't really know what else to say."

I looked down at her, swallowing hard. "I think I should be the one thanking you." And then I rolled out of bed and pulled on my clothes. It was hard to walk away, but I knew it would be harder to stay. We both needed time to think about what had happened and what we were going to do about it.

I had just made love to Harmony Wynham. I'd made love to the woman I had fallen in love with when I hadn't been looking. And, yes, she had cried.

And I had no idea what I was going to do about it.

By the time I went home, showered, and made my way to the bar, my mind was in total disarray. I kept talking myself out of wanting another date with Harmony. It was almost like if I were to take her out again, I risked hurting her. But then I would make her feel as if we had done something wrong. And we didn't.

Not when it was between us.

But it was all piling up so much, and I couldn't focus on anything. I needed to talk it out, but I didn't think I was going to be able to do that today. Not when I knew we had another wing night, and I didn't know when I would have some private time with Harmony again to figure it out.

Plus, I needed time on my own to figure things out before I spoke with her.

Because I refused to hurt her.

Even if I was afraid that I might have already done so.

Beckham was behind the bar when I got there, and he gave me a nod. We were open for lunch in another ten minutes, so I knew that Aiden was probably there, as well.

Cameron wasn't working until later, but I had the books to go over, and then a few phone calls to make to ensure that the next pool tournament was ready to go. I had piles and piles of paperwork to go through, and I didn't even know who was on staff for the day. I'd been so in my head regarding my own problems, that I'd let things fall to the wayside.

I couldn't do that.

"Hey, you look well rested," Beckham said, giving me a look.

I knew I had bags under my eyes, and I likely looked nothing like a well-rested man. That's what happened when you stayed up too late making love to the woman you knew you shouldn't have. Even if I should.

"Shut up."

"So, your date with Harmony went well last night, then?"

"I'm really not going to talk about it with you."

"Good. Harmony deserves her privacy. But I just wanted to let you know I'm happy for the two of you. It's about time."

I just looked at the other man and shook my head. "Really? About time?"

"Don't tell me you're having second thoughts."

"I think I'm having third or fourth thoughts."

"You're going to fuck this up and hurt her if you keep

having those types of thoughts," Beckham said, folding his arms over his chest.

"Well, I can't help it. There's a lot of thoughts to have when it comes to the two of us. We don't come baggage-free."

Beckham just shook his head. "Nobody our age is baggage-free. Hell, no one *any* age is baggage-free these days. We all have shit in our pasts that we have to overcome. That's what makes us human. But the two of you? You fit. And, yeah, it's not easy, and there's a lot of layers that will get messy, but the two of you can wade through it. You're both thinkers. Sometimes that's great, and sometimes it means you overthink shit. So, just talk to your woman and figure it out. Because I see the way she looks at you, and I see the way you try not to look at her. You two are good for each other. You're not going to mess it up. Unless you think too much. So don't think."

"That's not very helpful," I said, even though that wasn't quite true. "I said I'm a thinker. I can't help *but* think."

"Just don't think stupidly."

I rolled my eyes and flipped him off. "Thanks for that."

"Well, I'm a bartender. I'm pretty good at helping."

"I hate you," I said, laughing.

"Well, I tried."

I was still laughing as the door opened, and I looked over to see who had come in. We weren't open for another ten minutes or so, so I was surprised to see anyone walking in.

And then everything froze, and I swallowed hard.

Of course. Of course, when I was trying to get my thoughts in order would be when he showed up.

Of course.

"Sam," I said, my voice a growl.

Out of the corner of my eye, I watched Beckham roll his shoulders back and glare at the other man, folding his arms over his chest.

I wasn't alone here, and I was grateful for that, but I really didn't want to get into this today.

Suddenly, Aiden was behind the bar as well, and Dillon and Cameron came out from the office area. I hadn't even known they were back there. I'd only been here for a few minutes, and already everything was going to shit.

Sam stood in the doorway, a few steps in, the light glowing behind him as if the man were an angel.

He was anything but, and it didn't matter how many steps Sam went through to change.

There was nothing angelic about him.

The man just looked at me, and I knew if I didn't talk,

if I didn't just listen, I'd have to deal with him later. It might as well be today.

"I'm sorry to bother you. I wanted to come in before you opened if you happened to be here so I didn't bother anyone." Sam said the words quickly, not slurred but precise as if he were thinking about each word carefully.

I didn't know what to say. I didn't know if I had words at all. And then everything became just that more outrageous as another person walked in behind Sam.

Harmony looked between us, her eyes narrowed, and then she came from around Sam and walked directly towards me.

She didn't kiss me, didn't touch me, and I was glad for that. I wasn't sure what I would do if she did any of that. Instead, she stood right behind me to my side, in front of Dillon and beside Cameron. My whole family was there, and so was Harmony, standing by my side. I knew that I wasn't alone.

I really didn't want Harmony to see this.

I didn't want her to see this part of my past. I'd washed it away with each shower to get clean. I had my go-bag at my house, for fuck's sake.

All of that in case things went to hell.

And I had taken a step in my life last night that would forever change things.

But now my past was facing me, literally—to try and make amends, most likely.

"What can I do for you, Sam?"

Sam wrung his hands in front of himself and took a deep breath. "I'd like to speak with you for a few moments if you don't mind. Do you have somewhere we can talk in private?"

I shook my head, folding my arms across my chest.

"My family's here, Sam. You can say what you want." I saw the other man flinch, and I felt bad about it.

I shouldn't. I shouldn't feel anything for him. But I didn't want to hurt him. I didn't want to be an asshole.

I didn't want to feel *anything*. But it was hard not to feel when this man was in front of me, reminding me of what he had done, of who I had been.

And Harmony was here to witness it. The one person I didn't want to see that part of me, even though she already knew. Having the facts, and then having them thrown in your face was something different completely.

"Okay. I can do that. I'm here to tell you I'm sorry. I'm sorry for the man I was. I'm not that person anymore. But you don't have to believe that. I'm sorry for what I did. And I'm sorry I wasn't there for you. I'm sorry we lost your ma, and that I did nothing to help with that. I apologize about the drinking. The drugs. I'm sorry for not giving you a home or a roof over your head. And I'm sorry for what I did after. For not being your dad. Because I wasn't. I'm not. I don't have that right. Those people that took you in? They have that right. And I apologize that I missed out on telling them thank you for taking you in, for being the parents I couldn't be. So, I'm sorry, Brendon, I'm sorry for everything."

I looked at Sam, and I didn't feel anger, not the type I thought I should have. Instead, there was just an empty hollowness. There was nothing there.

It reminded me of the shell of myself that I'd had to become in order to live when I was younger.

And I hated him for it.

But worse, I hated myself.

"Okay. I forgive you."

I noticed the others straighten just slightly at that. Even Sam's eyes widened.

"I forgive you because you look clean. And I know you went through hell. But so did I. So, I forgive you, but I can't forget. That means I can't have you in my life. I hope you get that."

I was a bastard. Someone else might have been able to let Sam back into their life. Someone else might have been strong. But I wasn't. I couldn't. I couldn't forget what had happened. I could forgive him because it's what he needed, but I couldn't forget enough to look at him every day and be who I needed to be to survive.

And maybe that would be my amends later, but that was my decision to make.

I just hated the fact that the others had to see this.

"I get that, Brendon. Thank you for letting me speak. I'll leave you alone now. I'll never come back. Never bother you again. I'm glad that you have the life you need. I'm glad you got that. I wish you all the success in everything you have and do."

And with that, my father walked out of my life. Most likely for the last time. The first time, the second time, and even the fifth time he had walked away...I didn't remember them. Not really. It was all so faded, though it probably should have been crisp from all the pain.

But I felt like this would be the last time.

As the others looked at me, I suddenly couldn't feel anything, only disgust. Anger.

Because that was the man who had tried to raise me even though he hadn't at all.

That was the past I came from.

Harmony was quiet, and I turned to her.

Tears filled her eyes, those fucking tears—just like the night before.

So, when she put her hand on my chest, the others looked away, giving me privacy even though there wasn't much space for that.

"Brendon," she whispered, but I shook my head.

I moved back, took a step away from her. Because I couldn't let her touch me right now. I couldn't let her look at me.

I had to do what I swore I would never do. I had to walk away. Because I was only going to hurt her. I would always be the boy who had been sold on the streets. I was the guy who wasn't good enough.

I would always be second best.

But that's where I deserved to be.

"I'm sorry. I can't do this. I can't be the person you need me to be." As her eyes widened, and she took a step back, I heard one of my brothers curse under his breath. I didn't know which one it was, and I didn't care just then. Instead, I moved past them all, my shoulder shoving hard into Aiden's as I walked back to the office.

Everything was so fucked-up.

And I'd just made a mistake.

Probably the biggest of my life.

But I had no idea what the fucking hell to do.

I was Brendon Connolly.

I didn't deserve Harmony.

I didn't deserve anything.

CHAPTER EIGHTEEN

I might be small, but I am mighty. Don't forget my wrath.

- Harmony in a text to Brendon

HARMONY

I STOOD THERE TRANSFIXED. That could not have just happened.

No. That did not just happen.

I looked to where Brendon had walked and blinked, trying to slow down my breathing.

I was not just rejected. Not after I had given myself to Brendon.

He was simply hurting, confused.

He just had to get over himself and get through his feelings, and then we could deal.

I fisted my hands at my sides and took a step towards the hallway, but Cameron stood in my way.

I looked up at him, the man who was in love with my best friend, the sister of my heart, and glared.

"You're going to want to get out of my way right now, Cameron Connolly."

Cameron just sighed and shook his head. "Harmony, why don't you give him some space? I'll go talk with him, and we'll figure out what's going on."

"I don't think so. You're going to move out of my way, and I'm going to go talk with him. Now."

"He's going through a lot, Harmony."

I looked over at Aiden and raised my chin. "I know. And I'm going to talk him through it. Because in case you two haven't realized it, I care for your brother. And I'm going to help him. He's the one who just told me that he couldn't do this. That he thinks he can't be the person I need him to be. So this is between us. I know exactly what just happened, and I'm going to go fix it. And you two will get out of my way, or I'll kick you both in the balls. Then you'll really have to deal with me. I'm not weak.

Not spineless where you can just push me out of the way."

Dillon cleared his throat and grinned before taking a dramatic step to the side. "Oh, I know you can handle it. Just know that we're here for you if you need us. If he gets grouchy or annoying, call for us, and we'll be right in there."

I looked at the youngest Connolly that wasn't quite a Connolly yet. "Listen to the youngster. He seems to be the only one who knows what he's talking about."

I knew I was acting a little bitchy. I was taking my anger and my hurt out on them, but I didn't know what else to do. I was in pain, and I needed to talk with Brendon. Honestly, I knew he was hurting, too. He had lashed out, but I wouldn't let him continue lashing out at me.

That was not how these things worked.

On my way up the stairs to the office, I rolled my shoulders back even though my hands shook.

I knew this wasn't just about me, it was about so much more. Brendon was going through so much, and I knew he didn't always handle it well.

I had always known that. It wasn't new. But I was here to help. I had been before, and I was going to be even more so now.

Having to say those things to his father? To tell him that he forgave him but that Sam couldn't be part of his life? That had to have hurt. On top of the fact that I knew we were both reeling about what had happened the night before.

It was likely too much. So much that it was hard for me to even fully comprehend it. And I only knew parts.

So, we were going to handle this.

I opened the office door and found Brendon staring out the window, both hands curled into fists above his head on either side of the pane.

He looked so sad, so broken.

All I wanted to do was gather him up in my arms and tell him that everything was going to be okay. But I knew better than most that everything wasn't okay all the time. Sometimes, you had to get through the non-okay parts before you could breathe again.

We were going to do that. Together, damn it.

"That's not how this works, Brendon," I said, not knowing exactly what I was going to say until I said it.

He turned to me and didn't even stiffen. He had known I was there, but he hadn't looked at me. He turned back to the window.

It hurt, but it shouldn't. Because Brendon was hurting, and I was going to be there for him. He was always there for me, no matter what. No matter how he was feeling, he was always there for me.

So, I was going to be there for him. But first, we

needed to get a few things out of the way. "We're going to talk, Brendon. We're going to talk about what happened down there—with Sam, with me, with you. We're going to talk. Because you don't get to walk away like that. Do you hear me? You don't get to walk away when it hurts. We talk about it. That's how it's always been. And it's going to stay that way. Okay?"

He didn't turn again, so I walked forward and put my hands on his back. I wasn't afraid that he would turn and hurt me. I was never scared of that. It didn't matter that he had violence in his past, he'd never been violent towards anyone in his life.

I wasn't afraid of him. I might be scared of what could happen if he walked away, if he pushed me out of his life forever, but I wasn't going to think about that.

Because we would get through this.

"I'm not the right person, Harmony. I'm not the person I need to be for you. Don't you see that? Of course, you do. You cried."

I froze and blinked. But he still wasn't looking at me. I wished he would look at me.

"You mean last night? When we made love for the first time?"

"You know what I mean. You cried. I hurt you. And I refuse to do that again. So you need to leave. You need to leave before I hurt you any more than I already have."

I swallowed the lump in my throat and tugged on the back of his shirt. "You're going to hurt me if you don't look at me. So look at me, Brendon. Face me and let's talk about it. That's what we do. We talk. We don't hide our feelings. You let me breathe, you let me heal. So let me help you do that, too. Face me. Talk to me about it. Be the man I know you are. Not the man you *think* you are."

He was so still for so long, I was afraid he would never turn, that everything would be lost. That no matter how hard I fought, he wouldn't fight for us.

But then his shoulders sagged just for a moment before they stiffened again and he turned.

I didn't touch him then, knowing that he likely needed space even though I didn't want to give him too much.

I wanted to reach out. I wanted to lay my hands on his skin and feel him, to know that he was real. And for him to know I was real, too.

But I didn't.

Not yet.

You cried," he said, his voice soft.

"Of course, I did. It was the first time I'd had sex with someone other than Moyer. Moyer wasn't my first, but he was my only for a long time. And then I was having sex with you. Making love with you. And it was wonderful, and it was perfect, and I wasn't thinking about him then.

I was thinking about all the emotions running through me because I was with *you*. It was just you and me, like we said. It was us. So, yes, I cried. Because I'm an emotional wreck sometimes, and I cry. You know that. You know I cry at puppy commercials, and TV shows that even mention a puppy. I cry when someone wins the lottery when they've been down on their luck. I cried when your brother got a new beer. He was so happy that it made him smile and pick up Violet and dance around the room. I cried because they were happy. I just cry sometimes. I wasn't hurt. I wasn't thinking about Moyer. I promise."

Brendon looked at me then, his eyes devoid of emotion, but I knew it was just a façade. He was holding back everything because it was all a bit too much.

I knew Brendon. Even if I hadn't realized exactly what my feelings were until this moment. I *knew* Brendon.

"You had to watch what happened. You had to look at me and watch me push away the man who tried to raise me."

"No, that wasn't what you did. You told me before what Sam did to you. I've never seen someone as strong as you were just then. And you know how much I hate the word *strong*."

His lips quirked into a smile then, and I felt like we

277

were one step closer to winning. "I know you hate that word."

"Of course, I do. Even though it's a good one. It means so much, and that's why it's difficult to hear. But you did exactly what you felt you needed to do, and I will always support you. Even before we were what we are together now, I would've supported you. Because you did what you needed to do for yourself and for that man. He came here for atonement, and he got it. You didn't have to give him anything else. You didn't have to give him what you *did*. And I know it was hard, and we can talk about it more later. I promise. Anything you want to talk about, I am here for you. I'm sorry that you went through any of that at all. That you had to feel that. But you're here now. You have your brothers. You have me. Us. Just know that you're loved. And you're not alone. You'll never be alone again."

"I hated him for so long," Brendon said softly. I stood there, wanting to reach out but knowing if I moved, if I breathed too loudly, he could stop talking. I needed him to keep talking.

"I hated him. And I felt like I was nothing because of him. It took me a while to be who I am now, and I know I'm not perfect. But, Harmony? I'm not sure I'm the right person for you. Because while I can get over what Sam did to me, and I can get over what happened to me as a kid because I've been working on getting through it my entire teenage and adult life, seeing him brought it all back. But that's not the only thing on my mind. It's the future. It's looking at you, knowing that I love you and I'm afraid you'll look at me and see what you don't have anymore. That's why I'm afraid."

It didn't hurt, it wasn't a slap across the face, but it was still an echo of pain.

I'd spent so much of my life trying not to put labels on myself, and it was odd to think that my future was staring at me and not seeing exactly who I'd become. But maybe it was just because I hadn't said it enough. Or well enough. Perhaps it was because I had allowed him to take care of me for so long that he couldn't see what I had strived so hard for.

So, I'd make that change happen.

"That's not how this works," I said again, my voice soft but strong. I cleared my throat, making sure I was a little louder this time. "I remember what it felt like with Moyer. That's my past. He will always be in my memories, and I will always love him. And you know that. Just like you'll always love him, as well. But I also know how it feels when I'm with you."

I looked up at him and made sure that he understood that what I was saying was the truth.

"I'm allowed another happily ever after. That's my

right. I'm allowed to love again. I'm allowed to put myself out there and know that it's okay not to be okay and yet be okay. So you don't get to push me away when it hurts, when you're afraid that I'm not seeing you the way I should. Because I do. And you know why? Because I'm your friend. I have always been that, and over the past few months, we've gotten even closer. I let you into my bed. In my body. Inside my heart."

My voice broke then, and he reached out to touch my face. I leaned into his hold and wanted to close my eyes and cry. Because that's what I did. I cried. I hadn't cried often, not since everything had changed. But I was past that now. So, I cried. But there wouldn't be any more tears today. Only truths.

"I let you into my heart," I repeated. "So, you don't get to run when it hurts. And I don't get to either." I took a deep breath. "So, you should probably know that I've already fallen in love with you, even though we both know it's too soon and we shouldn't. But there it is. You just said you loved me, and we'll just blow past that because it's a lot, and we're still trying to figure out exactly what we are to each other. And that's fine. But, yes, I love you. It's probably too soon. And, no, it's not the same love that it was when we were just friends. But I don't think it has been for a while. It's a love that grows. And I love you. So now, what are you going to do about it? What are you going to do about us? Because I'm here, Brendon. And I'm not going anywhere."

I rolled back my shoulders and just looked at him, praying that I hadn't laid my heart out for nothing.

And then his eyes darkened, and he lowered his face to mine. It was just a soft kiss, a brush of lips against mine. "You are fucking amazing, Harmony. I knew you were amazing before, but right now? You're a goddess. My own personal Wonder Woman."

"I could use the Lasso of Truth right about now," I whispered against his lips, and he laughed and then kissed me hard.

And then, suddenly, his hands were in my hair, and my arms were around his body. And then his hands were below my butt, picking me up. I wrapped my legs around his waist, and then my back was suddenly against the door.

We were in his office with his family right downstairs, but we didn't care.

There was a clash of teeth and tongues and heavy breathing.

All I knew was that I needed him inside me. I needed his touch, needed *him*.

He worked the button on my pants, and I tried to do the same for him, but I couldn't make it work.

My legs were still around his waist even as he stripped

me out of my clothes and he did the same with his, and then my pants were gone, and he was inside of me, warm, bare—something we would need to talk about later, but that was fine. Because it didn't matter.

This was Brendon, and he would always make sure I was safe.

And then there were no words, no thoughts, just hard and hot against the door. It banged, loud and fast, and we made love, fucked right there—something I had always wanted to do.

This was his office, his domain, and I was his. Taken, claimed. Brendon's.

And when we both came, panting as we tried to call out each other's names, I leaned into him, trying to catch my breath.

"I fucking love you," he growled.

"I love you, too. Wow," I said, my voice breathy.

"Wow, indeed. And I'm pretty sure everyone just heard that," Brendon said, laughing, still inside me.

"Yeah. I don't know how I'm going to face them later, but whatever. Don't do that again, Brendon."

He looked up at me, blinking. "Don't fuck you against the door again?"

"No, you can do that anytime. Maybe when I'm wearing a dress so it's a little easier. Pants were difficult."

"Yeah, dresses would be easier. And we didn't use a condom."

"I know, but I'm on birth control, and I'm clean."

"Me, too. But we probably should've been safer about that. I'll never hurt you. Never again. I might get too far into my head at times and try to protect you from myself, but that's just because I can't stop wanting to make sure that you are safe and cared for."

I cupped his face and kissed him softly, in love with the man that had been my friend for as long as I could remember. And he would always be that, even as our love grew into something more, something vivid.

"You're mine, Brendon Connolly. Always."

"Always. I promise."

And I trusted that promise with everything that I was. Maybe someone else wouldn't, perhaps it was too soon for some people, but I knew love, and I knew destiny and fate and all of that. I knew that sometimes taking a chance when no one else would was the only way to truly understand what love and fate and all of that was and what it meant.

Because Brendon had always been a part of my life, I just somehow ignored the fact that my love had grown for him in a different way.

But I was never going to ignore it again.

No matter what.

EPILOGUE

---

*I'll take care of her. I promise. Thank you for loving
her first.*

- Brendon to Moyer. Today.

BRENDON

I WAS A MESS. Life was a mess. But I was happy. That
didn't really sound like it should all make sense together,
but it did. Because, yeah, just because I was a healthy,
emotionally-mature adult, that didn't mean my life was

perfect. It was so far from that, yet sometimes it felt exactly how it needed to be.

I was in love with my best friend, with a woman who made me smile, who challenged me, and who somehow, through some fate I still did not understand, loved me back.

What more could I want?

Yeah, I probably could've asked for an easier childhood. I could've probably gone without ever seeing Sam again in my life. But that was all behind me. I was strong.

A word I knew Harmony hated, but we were both getting through it.

I didn't think I would ever see Sam again, but if I did, I knew I'd be able to deal with it because of Harmony.

Maybe, one day, I would *want* to see him. Get to know him. If I did, I'd hire a private detective and find my way through that. But I honestly didn't think that would happen.

I'd had my parents. Jack and Rose were everything to me, and I hated that they were gone. I missed them more each and every day. But they had raised me. Cameron and Aiden were my brothers regardless if we shared blood.

And Dillon was my brother, too, even if he was still new to me, and I was just starting to get to know this kid who was a bright font of knowledge and grace.

The women in my life were amazing, and the depth of

their emotions and strength just told me that I would never be truly alone again.

Violet, Sienna, and even Meadow would always make me laugh. They would forever be little sisters to me, even if Meadow was a little newer to the game.

Same as Beckham. The quiet, mysterious guy who liked to make me laugh and make fun of me—he was in my life, too.

I wasn't alone.

And I would never be alone when it came to Harmony either.

She had chosen me, given herself to me, even as I had given myself to her.

And I wasn't allowed to walk away again.

Even if I'd only done it for a moment because I thought it was for her own good. I was never allowed to do it again.

I can still remember the hurt in her voice, the pain in her eyes when I finally looked at her again that day in the office. I knew that she was my everything and that I could never walk away again—even if it was only in a fit of emotion.

My life wasn't in shambles, it was pretty damn put-together. It just took me a while to see that. Everyone around me were the same people they had been before I finally made that leap with Harmony, but it was as if knowing that I could take a chance had allowed me to lean on them at the same time. It had opened my eyes to the idea that they were there, that I wasn't alone. And I had the woman I'd always thought I shouldn't have, the one who would be in my life for as long as I could have it happen.

Because I knew forevers weren't always a promise. Not with everything we'd all been through. But I would love Harmony until the end of my days. And I would do everything in my power to make sure she understood that. She had saved me from myself, and I would always be there for her.

I had my family, my woman, my bar, my business, and my life.

It might be a lot, but it was pretty fucking amazing.

An arm wrapped around my waist, and I looked down at Harmony. "Are you just going to stand there and look pensive and broody all night? Not that you're not hot, but I need you to focus. We have a reputation to live up to. And a dance." She grinned at me, and my heart lurched. Fucking lurched.

Who was I?

I hardly recognized myself these days.

I laughed and kissed her on the tip of the nose before taking the pool cue out of her hand.

We weren't running a full tournament as that would

start the next night. However, we were doing tournament practice at the bar. We were decently busy, but it was the Connollys playing against each other while the newer members of the staff worked the front of the house. We pitched in, but the Connollys were doing PR first.

Only it really wasn't all the Connollys since Aiden and Sienna hadn't shown up to play. That was a little odd, but no one seemed really worried, other than the fact that the two might strangle each other if they were together. We didn't know if they *were* actually together since they hadn't said as much, but the two didn't say much of anything to us when it came to what they were thinking these days.

"We're going to kick Beckham's and Meadow's asses, don't worry," I said, laughing.

"I think that fake bartender over there means war," Beckham said to Meadow, and the quiet woman just laughed and rolled her eyes.

Beckham and Meadow were the ringers for the night since Aiden and Sienna hadn't shown up.

Both had texted that they wouldn't be there, claiming some excuse or another, but all of us thought it was odd, and we all had questions. Not that we could actually ask them since every time we brought up one of them to the other, they got all weird and yelled about it.

But it was fine. It was life.

And I had another woman to focus on, the one at my side.

Everyone watched and laughed and played around as I lined up my shot, knowing that I had to be really good at this since Meadow and Beckham were actually pretty decent pool players. I didn't think Harmony and I were actually going to win this time, mostly because we kept getting distracted by each other and kept making out in the corner rather than playing the game. But I wouldn't mind losing because of that. It actually sounded pretty damn good to me.

I hit the four into the corner pocket, but missed the next shot, cursing under my breath. I missed because Harmony had stood right beside me, and I could feel the heat of her.

I knew she hadn't done it on purpose, but it was all I could do not to pull her into my arms and throw her onto the pool table so I could have my way with her. That probably wouldn't be the best thing to do, though.

"Are you guys just going to keep making moo-moo eyes at each other?" Dillon asked from my side as the kid started busing some of the tables. He was the only one of us actually working tonight, so we all stepped in behind the bar. Okay, the rest of them stepped in behind the bar. Beckham wouldn't let me. Whatever. I tried to help.

"I don't really think that's the saying," Harmony said, laughing.

Dillon just shrugged. "Whatever. Moo-moo eyes, cow eyes, moon eyes. You keep looking at each other and making out when you don't think anyone's looking, even though we're all looking. Not that I'm not happy for you guys, but come on. Do we always have to watch that?"

The kid visibly shuddered, even though he was smiling, so I handed over the pool cue, pulled Harmony into my arms, and dipped her, kissing her hard, our lips meshing, leaving both of us panting. She wrapped her arms around my neck and kicked up one leg.

I saw the flash and knew Violet was taking a photo of us, so I dipped Harmony a little deeper and then pulled her up to her feet and spun her. I'd have to ask for that photo later. I'd want the damn thing framed.

Harmony laughed and fell against my chest while Dillon just rolled his eyes and stomped away, likely going to bus more tables.

I was so damn happy. Even though I'd never thought I could be this happy. I still didn't quite trust it, but I trusted the woman in my arms. We still had a ways to go, and even though we had told each other that we loved each other, we knew that love was going to change, deepen, just grow. We were going to move slowly in our relationship, slower than we had been, even though it seemed as if it had moved at full speed as soon as we allowed each other to look at one another in that way.

But we were going to get to know each other again and find the new parts of ourselves.

And I was ready for that.

I knew there would be days when we would both be reminded of what we lost, but we would have each other for that. I knew that Harmony had already talked to both of her parents, and they were oddly supportive of the relationship. Maybe it was because they knew me, so it made things easier. Regardless, as long as Harmony was fine, I was good.

I was surrounded by my family, joined by the woman that trusted me to love her and trusted me with her love. There would likely be issues that arose. Even though the bar was doing great, it could go bad at any moment. Because that was just the name of the game. I was still working too hard, and I would have to find a way to fix things there. Maybe I'd actually trust more people at my other job and work more at the bar because I wanted to be near my family and friends.

Maybe I'd learn to delegate.

Harmony still needed to work as many hours as she did at her charity, and I wanted to find a way to help her with that, even though I knew she could handle everything on her own. I just wanted to be a part of it.

I knew that we didn't have a normal relationship, but there was nothing normal about anything having to do with us. We had all been through hell, but we had found our way through.

I was holding the one woman I shouldn't have, and yet she was the person I wanted, the one I loved.

There was no holding back about it. Not anymore.

"You look pensive again," Harmony said as she leaned into me. I kissed her, knowing that Dillon was still around, as were the others.

"I'll try to be better."

"Oh, I don't mind you all broody. A broody Brendon is kind of sexy."

"Well, I think I can keep brooding if you want me to." I swallowed hard, remembering how I'd wanted to touch her like this the last time we played and had held myself back. We'd only been friends then. At least on the surface. It had taken looking beneath that layer to find who we truly were to each other. "I love you," I whispered, kissing her again. "Thank you for taking a chance on me. Thank you for saying yes."

She looked up at me, smiling, so much love and trust in her eyes that it was hard for me to keep my emotions at bay. And for someone who used to be so good at keeping everything locked down, that was surprising.

"I love you, too. Thanks for holding me. And just for

being here. And thanks for being you."

I knew she meant that. Because the funny thing was, with her, I saw the path I could take. I knew that when I looked in my past, I didn't have to fret about everything that kept coming at me.

With Harmony, I didn't need to go back. Hold back. I didn't need to wake up with cold sweats anymore. Oh, they would probably return because that was my life. But it wasn't the *only* part of my life.

Harmony was the major part. And so was my family.

I was happy, something I hadn't let myself be for a while.

I kissed Harmony again and then grinned as the others cheered since Beckham had sunk the eight ball, officially beating us in the practice pool tournament.

There would be no dancing tonight, or maybe there would be, but only in private.

Because I had my Harmony...and I couldn't wait to see our next dance.

Next in the Fractured Connections series:

FALLING WITH YOU

A NOTE FROM CARRIE ANN RYAN

Thank you so much for reading **SHOULDN'T HAVE YOU.** I do hope if you liked this story, that you would please leave a review! Reviews help authors *and* readers.

This story wasn't easy to write. That's an understatement. I knew I needed to write it but I didn't know it would feel...like this in the end. I hope you loved Harmony and Brendon's story even if it's a little different. They both had to come to terms with what was while finding their friendship first.

This series is heavy, I know that, but in the end, there is hope, there is that happily ever after. I wanted to write a series where there is love even when it doesn't feel like there can be.

I'm honored you're reading this series and I do hope

you continue on. This is possibly one of my most personal series and I'm blessed in the fact I get to write it.

Next up is Sienna and Aiden and they have some explaining to do. And Meadow and Beckham surprised me and screamed that they needed their stories as well.

If you missed Cameron and Violet's story, it's called Breaking Without You and out now!

BTW, in case you didn't know, Mace and Adrienne had their story in Fallen Ink as the Fractured Series is part of the Montgomery Ink world!

And if you're new to my books, you can start anywhere within the my interconnected series and catch up! Each book is a stand alone, so jump around!

Don't miss out on the Montgomery Ink World!

- Montgomery Ink (The Denver Montgomerys)
- Montgomery Ink: Colorado Springs (The Colorado Springs Montgomery Cousins)
- Montgomery Ink: Boulder (The Boulder Montgomery Cousins)
- Gallagher Brothers (Jake's Brothers from Ink Enduring)
- Whiskey and Lies (Tabby's Brothers from Ink Exposed)
- Fractured Connections (Mace's sisters from Fallen Ink)

ABOUT THE AUTHOR

Carrie Ann Ryan is the New York Times and USA Today bestselling author of contemporary and paranormal romance. Her works include the Montgomery Ink, Redwood Pack, Talon Pack, and Gallagher Brothers series, which have sold over 2.0 million books worldwide. She started writing while in graduate school for her advanced degree in chemistry and hasn't stopped since. Carrie Ann has written over fifty novels and novellas with more in the works. When she's not writing about bearded tattooed men or alpha wolves that need to find their mates, she's reading as much as she can and exploring the world of baking and gourmet cooking.

www.CarrieAnnRyan.com

MORE FROM CARRIE ANN RYAN

Montgomery Ink: Colorado Springs
Book 1: Fallen Ink
Book 2: Restless Ink
Book 2.5: Ashes to Ink
Book 3: Jagged Ink
Book 3.5: Ink by Numbers

The Fractured Connections Series:
A Montgomery Ink Spin Off Series
Book 1: Breaking Without You
Book 2: Shouldn't Have You
Book 3: Falling With You
Book 4: Taken With You

The Montgomery Ink: Boulder Series:

Book 1: Wrapped in Ink

Book 2: Sated in Ink

The Less Than Series:
A Montgomery Ink Spin Off Series

Book 1: Breathless With Her

Book 2: Reckless With You

Book 3: Shameless With Him

The Elements of Five Series:

Book 1: From Breath and Ruin

Book 2: From Flame and Ash

Montgomery Ink:

Book 0.5: Ink Inspired

Book 0.6: Ink Reunited

Book 1: Delicate Ink

Book 1.5: Forever Ink

Book 2: Tempting Boundaries

Book 3: Harder than Words

Book 4: Written in Ink

Book 4.5: Hidden Ink

Book 5: Ink Enduring

Book 6: Ink Exposed

Book 6.5: Adoring Ink

Book 6.6: Love, Honor, & Ink

Book 7: Inked Expressions

Book 7.3: Dropout

Book 7.5: Executive Ink

Book 8: Inked Memories

Book 8.5: Inked Nights

Book 8.7: Second Chance Ink

The Gallagher Brothers Series:
A Montgomery Ink Spin Off Series

Book 1: Love Restored

Book 2: Passion Restored

Book 3: Hope Restored

The Whiskey and Lies Series:
A Montgomery Ink Spin Off Series

Book 1: Whiskey Secrets

Book 2: Whiskey Reveals

Book 3: Whiskey Undone

The Talon Pack:

Book 1: Tattered Loyalties

Book 2: An Alpha's Choice

Book 3: Mated in Mist

Book 4: Wolf Betrayed

Book 5: Fractured Silence

Book 6: Destiny Disgraced

Book 7: Eternal Mourning
Book 8: Strength Enduring
Book 9: Forever Broken

Redwood Pack Series:

Book 1: An Alpha's Path
Book 2: A Taste for a Mate
Book 3: Trinity Bound
Redwood Pack Box Set (Contains Books 1-3)
Book 3.5: A Night Away
Book 4: Enforcer's Redemption
Book 4.5: Blurred Expectations
Book 4.7: Forgiveness
Book 5: Shattered Emotions
Book 6: Hidden Destiny
Book 6.5: A Beta's Haven
Book 7: Fighting Fate
Book 7.5: Loving the Omega
Book 7.7: The Hunted Heart
Book 8: Wicked Wolf
The Complete Redwood Pack Box Set (Contains Books 1-7.7)

The Branded Pack Series:
(Written with Alexandra Ivy)

Book 1: Stolen and Forgiven

CPSIA information can be obtained
at www.ICGtesting.com
Printed in the USA
FSHW021138030120
65704FS